CLAIMED IN CHAOS

CKMC4
LINNY LAWLESS

CHAOS KINGS
MOTORCYCLE CLUB

To Anita

Linny Lawless

Cover Models: Jamie Walker & Ivy Edinger
Photographer: Reggie Deanching
Cover Design: Cosmic Letterz Cover Design
PA Services: Mikki Thomas
Editor: Darice Gamble
Formatting: Dandelion Designs

To Jeanette

My long-time book worm friend

PROLOGUE

MAGNET

"You're not backing out of this, Magnet. You already promised Sam." Ratchet took a drag off his smoke. He had daggers in his eyes as he glared at me.

"Who is she again?" I asked.

Ratchet exhaled and rolled his eyes. "Sam's friend Kat. They work together over at the used bookstore. She's been here at the clubhouse a few times."

"The one with the purple hair?"

I remembered meeting Kat before. She was cute. The last time I saw her, she had purple hair and wore glasses. I could never quite make out the shape of her body (was she curvy? was she petite?) because she always wore long flowy skirts.

I glanced at Becky and Brandy, who were both leaning their asses up against the pool table near the jukebox. They weren't going to like the idea of another chick riding on the back of my chopper.

"Yeah. Ok." I nodded my head towards them. "I just gotta break the news to my girls."

Wez chuckled, standing there, his boulder-sized biceps crossed over his chest. "You're such a fuckin' slut, Magnet. Who's the boss in this threesome jamboree you got goin' on? You? or them?"

Ratchet smashed his cigarette in one of the big glass ashtrays and climbed off the barstool. "Whatever you need to do, Magnet. Just make it happen. Kat's a nice girl and she's a good friend of Sam's." He sauntered over and socked me right in the shoulder with his southpaw jab. "And don't fuck around with her. You got your two B's over there for that."

* * *

Becky rode my face, and Brandy rode my cock the night before. They both knew how to have fun and were kinky as fuck. Sometimes they'd hiss and get into little cat fights over who got to ride on my bike, so I made them play rock-paper-scissors to decide. Becky had platinum blond hair and a delicious ass you just wanted to sink your teeth into. Brandy had hair like the color of honey. She had plenty of curves and a nice set of paid-for tits. The three of us together were just a hot bundle of sexy-as-fuck.

I was out of the shower and ready to get my day going, but the girls were still in my bed. I lunged and landed on the bed in between them, slapping their asses. "Time to rise and shine girls!"

Brandy groaned first, then Becky whimpered. They weren't going to budge. I knew they both were going to suffer through the day with hangovers. So I left them to sleep in my bed all day. I told them both last night about the break-out ride and about Kat. They pouted and whined a bit, so I reassured them that it's for a good cause. Besides - I couldn't back out of a favor I promised to one of my Chaos brothers and his ole lady. So, I climbed on my shovelhead and headed over to the bookstore to ask Kat out for this break-out ride.

CHAPTER ONE

KAT

I stuck my bottom lip out, blowing away the strand of hair that had come loose from my ponytail. I was frustrated with the new glasses that I just paid half my salary for. The new prescription lenses were giving me bad depth-perception and my eyes were still adjusting. It was late Sunday morning and the spring pollen really did a number on me as my eyes watered and my nose felt stuffed up. I turned the sign in the front window to OPEN and started my day by unpacking a full box of used Dean Koontz paperbacks. I climbed up the step ladder in the horror section, with mild vertigo. I had to reach up to the highest shelf to stack them in the right place.

I heard the distant rumble of a motorcycle just then, and it made me think about Sam and her big burly caveman of a biker, Ratchet, and sighed. I thought it was so hot to see them together and how Ratchet treated Sam like a pretty princess, the way she deserved to be treated. The jingle of the doorbell came to my ears then, waking me from my daydream of brutish bikers. A customer this early on a Sunday was typically a huge book worm (like me), wanting an enjoyable book to read on a nice spring Sunday afternoon. "Welcome to CC's used bookstore!" I called out, reaching up again with another Koontz book.

I bit my bottom lip as I reached up to place another book on the shelf, when my peripheral vision caught the sight of Magnet walking toward me. No, he wasn't walking. He was strutting toward me, looking just like a sexy erogenous pagan god! His light brown hair was long and tied back. His shoulders were so broad in a light denim blue tight ribbed tank top that matched the color of his eyes.

My jaw dropped as he came closer and closer toward me. My balance was off with the vertigo and the new glasses. And then it happened…in slow motion.

I cried out as I lost my balance, my long summer dress tangling up around my legs.

"I got you, Kitten." Magnet's deep voice was

music to my ears as I came crashing down on top of him, my chest smashing right onto his face.

Magnet's muscular arms wrapped around me as I gripped his broad shoulders. I slid down along his hard chest, until my feet touched the floor. But I had to lean my head back to look up. The corner of his mouth lifted, and I noticed a scruff of beard along his chiseled jaw. "Kat, right?"

I was numb with shock and embarrassment. My mouth hung open, "Yes." I stammered, "Thank you. I'm so sorry!"

His gorgeous head fell back as he let out a chuckle. "No apology needed kitten. Good thing I was here to catch you."

My nipples hardened instantly, just by him calling me kitten. I stepped back, out from within his hard, bulging biceps. I somehow managed to find my voice again. "Well thank you. It's Magnet, right?"

"Yep. That's the name my brothers gave me," he winked.

"How can I help you Magnet? Are you looking for a particular book or an author?"

He looked up at the shelf where I placed the Koontz books on, then his eyes roamed to the other bookshelf. Then back at me "I'm not here to buy any books. Takes up too much of my time to read. I wanted to invite you to our club's break-out ride. It's the first ride of the season. Its next weekend."

My heart skipped a beat. Ride? on a motorcycle? With Magnet? Oh, hell yeah!

"Sure!" I almost jumped up and down.

He laughed again, and his smile made my knees weak. "Ok then." Magnet's eyes roamed down my body and I suddenly felt embarrassed and blushed. "You can't ride wearing a dress or skirt. You'll need to wear some jeans and good riding boots."

"I can do that."

"Good. And a pair of shades. I have an extra helmet for you. You ever ridden on a motorcycle before?"

"Uh…no. But I learn quick."

"Ok good. So, you want me to pick you up at your place?"

"No. I can meet you at the Chaos King clubhouse if that's ok?"

"Sure. I'll meet you there at ten am next Saturday. "

I was so excited, my face ached at the smile I couldn't hide. "Thanks, Magnet. I'm really looking forward to it!"

He winked again "Yeah, me too kitten. See you then."

As Magnet sauntered back out of the bookstore, I waited a few seconds, then hurried to the front counter to watch him. He strapped his helmet on that hung from the handlebar and climbed back on his bright yellow chopper. His faded jeans hugged his solid thighs and hips. I just then, had an image of the V shape of those hips. I squeezed my thighs together and groaned. He put his shades on and started the motorcycle. The pipes roared to life. He twisted the throttle a few times, making the pipes thunder even louder. He shifted, twisting the throttle, and rolled out of the parking lot.

I didn't realize I was holding my breath until I exhaled loudly. Thank goodness I was alone and had no customers. I didn't know what it was about Magnet. I'm no virgin, of course…but there was something about him that made him so intriguing to me. He was the most gorgeous man I had ever seen.

I was sure that Magnet's invitation was Sam's idea. I had seen Magnet's girlfriends at the clubhouse before. They were all pretty and voluptuous, with that biker-chick look that I always tried to pull off, but could never quite get right. I was practically a hermit. I was sitting on the inside, looking out at the world around me. Like shaking a snow globe to watch the little tiny flecks of snow whirl around and fall down in a fantasy wonderland.

I was an obsessive book worm, reading books and living in another world in my imagination. I lived vicariously through the characters and worlds I read about. I was the complete opposite of my step-sister, Lillian. She was a gorgeous, successful, college graduate. I always felt like the boring ugly duckling next to her. My mother married Lillian's father when we were young teenagers. He suffered from a heart attack and died a few years ago. . I only saw my sister during holidays, weddings, or funerals.

* * *

I felt like I was floating on clouds, right up until Magnet left the parking lot. It was Easter Sunday, so my presence was expected at home, where I lived with my mother. As soon as I closed the bookstore later that afternoon, I headed home. I was already dressed for the occasion, wearing a flowy yellow dress with white daisies.

I was humming a tune to myself in the kitchen cutting stems on the two dozen daisies I had bought earlier. My mom rushed around the kitchen preparing for a big Easter dinner. "Guess who asked me out today mom?"

She was leaning down looking into the oven at the huge ham she was baking. She turned to look at me. "So that's why you look so pretty today! Who asked you out?"

"You know my friend Sam, right? And her boyfriend, Ratchet? Or James?"

"Yes, I do! That sweet friend of yours and that big and buff biker that dotes on her?"

"Yeah, they are a cute couple, aren't they? Well, do you remember me telling you about their motorcycle club, the Chaos Kings? One of them, the one they call Magnet, asked me out today!" I almost jumped again out of pure excitement.

"Oh, that good-looking beefcake you told me about?"

"Yes! Him!" we both squealed and giggled.

That's when Lillian arrived. She was dressed in a bold, bright pencil skirt with a cute blouse and stiletto heels. I instantly felt frumpy. She had that effect on me.

Lillian had chestnut-brown wavy hair with a perfect complexion, and one of those fake smiles that never quite seemed genuine. She gave me one of those hugs that was the standard holiday protocol "Pretty dress Katrina. Did you get it on sale?"

She always said things that sounded nice, but had a double-meaning that could be interpreted as rude, making me feel inferior to her.

"I actually bought this dress at the Second Chance thrift store in town."

Lillian shook her head slightly, with that fake smile, "Oh Kat. I hope you washed it first! I should take you where I go shopping – at the town center. Only the best designer-made clothes!"

I put on a smile, just as fake as hers, "I can't afford the kinds of clothes you wear Lilly. "

She winked at me. "Well, if you find yourself a rich boyfriend, maybe he could afford it for you! Problem solved!"

My mother, Jean, was there to help me get out of the awkward situation I found myself in with my materialistic stepsister. She held the pretty glass vase of daisies, "Well I just love her dress. There's not a lot of women that can pull off wearing yellow, like my Katrina can. And to match these beautiful daisies too!" She beamed a smile at me, not at Lillian. I loved my mother. She was my hero.

CHAPTER TWO

MAGNET

It was Saturday morning. I tied up my black riding boots, feeling like a nervous teenage boy going out on his first date. Ever since Kat fell on me last Sunday, I couldn't stop thinking about her! The feel of her plump soft tits smashing up against my face instantly made my dick hard. Then I caught the feminine scent of vanilla and flowers on her and I was fucken done for. She looked up at me through those black-rimmed glasses as I held her. An image quickly flashed in my brain of Kat on her knees, sucking my cock, and looking up at me wearing those same glasses.

I had no fucking idea why I called her Kitten. It just came to me the moment she cried out and I caught her. I usually liked a whole lot of cleavage and a nice pair of thighs on a woman. But the sight of Kat in that pretty yellow dress with flowers? It made my heart thump in my chest. What the fuck was wrong with me? I'd never really noticed her before at the clubhouse. I only knew she was a good friend of Sam's. She had purple hair the last time I saw her, but she must have washed it out to go back to her natural color: so dark it was almost black.

I'd bet she had more brain cells than me, Becky, and Brandy combined. But I made a promise I'd do this for Ratchet and Sam. And Ratchet was right. I've had my fair share of pussy: loose pussy, tight pussy, hairy pussy, shaved pussy, waxed pussy...all kinds. I had my girls anytime and anywhere I wanted.

I slapped my cheeks and raked my hands through my hair, *"You can do this. It's just a break-out ride for fucks sake!"*

The clubhouse lot was full as I rolled in. I spotted Kat instantly. "t*he Fuck*?" my bike lurched me forward suddenly, as I missed a gear downshifting. Everyone turned and looked, including Kat. She was dressed in tight-ass jeans that showed off her round curvy ass, with a very snug, neon orange tank top. Her plump tits were smashed together, displaying an amazing cleavage.

I was sure everyone could see the faint blush rising to my face as I planted me boots down and parked my bike next to Skully's. I climbed off, walking right to Kat. Her head titled, and her dark brown doe eyes were gazing right at me.

I opened my arms, "You wanna give me one of those nice tits-in-my-face hugs again, Kitten?"

Her breath hitched and then she giggled, "I wore my contacts today, so I won't be as clumsy this time." She came into my arms and I squeezed her. She was very short, and cute as a button. My damn dick slammed against the zipper of my jeans, before I could release her. *What the fuck was wrong with me!*

That's when Tanya, the cock-blocker, jumped and wrapped her arms around my shoulders, "My brother from a different mother!" I gave her a hug back, lifting her off her feet. She hissed in my ear, "behave today Noah. I'm watching you."

I rolled my eyes. I already got the lecture from Ratchet and his sucker punch to my shoulder about not fucking around with Kat. I released Tanya, as her ole man, Skully stood behind her, shrugging his shoulders.

"Hey Magnet! Can I sit on your bike?" Skully's son, Jake, stood beside Skully. His little hands were shoved into the front pockets of his jeans.

"Sure Jake!", I ruffled Mini-Skully on top of his head and he followed me over to my yellow chopper, his eyes glossed over with awe. He'd just started kindergarten and was bragging to all his friends about how his dad was a Chaos King and his friend Magnet had the coolest bike in the club. I agreed with little Jake too. My bike was a kick-ass ride.

I heaved him up under his arms and planted him onto the seat of my chopper.

I pulled my phone out, "I'll take some pics and send them to your dad. You can show them to your friends at school, little man."

He had a shit-eating grin on his face and gave me the double metal horns with his hands as I took some pics. Both Skully, Tanya, and all the Chaos Kings loved Jake. He pretty much cemented their relationship. For the first time in a long time, Tanya seemed happy and grounded.

I lifted Jake off my bike and he ran back to Skully. Kat stood with Tanya, her hip jutted out a bit in those tight-ass jeans that hugged every part of her. She was fucking gorgeous. And within the next few minutes, she'd be sitting on my bike, with her thighs hugging me.

Today's ride with the club was to break-in the Spring season and to look forward to the upcoming hot and hazy summer days. And I was going to break Kat in. On her first ride on a motorcycle. Everyone walked to their bikes, crushing out cigarettes and strapping on helmets.

"You ready for this Kat?" I asked her as she followed me to my bike. I unstrapped the extra helmet from the sissy bar and placed it on her head. Her doe eyes stared into mine as I clicked the strap into place under her chin.

I had to break eye contact and climb on the bike, as she fumbled to put her shades on. "Now climb on behind me, kitten. And anchor your boots on the foot begs back there."

When she climbed on, I waited a few seconds and anticipated the feel of her mouthwatering tits pressed up against my back. But it didn't happen. I swiveled my head toward her, "You're going to have to snuggle up to me Kitten. This is your first time, so wrap your arms around me. I'll be busy with the handlebars, so your hands can go wherever they want to."

"Well…if you say so." I looked down to see her arms come around me. Her little hands pressed onto my stomach. My dick jumped.

Kat squeaked next to my ear as I started my chopper and it roared to life. I revved the throttle a few times, in tune with the other thundering bikes. "You like that don't you? The sound? The vibrations on your ass, between your legs?"

She giggled, her chin resting on my shoulder, hugging me close, "Yeah! I do! Makes me horny!"

I chuckled. "Well hold on Kat, cause I'm about to pop your cherry!" Kat looked all prim and proper behind the glasses and long skirts. But that day, she looked like a sexy wildcat! The kind of woman I liked. The kind of woman I wanted to fuck.

I put on my shades and rolled out with my club. The Prez, Rocky, leading the pack, along with Spider, the VP. Ratchet and Gunner were usually the road captains, but since both Sam and Fiona were riding along, Shrek and a few other brothers took on those roles.

The Chaos Kings rode in a tight group out west, toward the Shenandoah mountains. Everything was in bloom all around us: the trees, the grass. Kat's soft little body clung onto me. After a full hour, the club made a pit stop to fill up. As we waited, I leaned back into her. Her arms came over my shoulders. It felt right. It felt natural.

"You want to climb off to stretch your legs?"

"No, I'm good. Right here." Kat's breath brushed across my ear, and my dick sprung to life again. Brandy and Becky got my dick hard, but not with the snap of a finger like Kat.

We rolled out again and pulled back into the clubhouse lot two hours later. Everyone climbed off bikes, unlatching lids and ready to throw down some liquor and light up some weed. But the moment Kat climbed off the bike, I was bummed the fuck out because I enjoyed the feeling her against me for two good hours.

"Are you going to hang out for a bit?" I sounded like a fucking dork. Me. The Chick Magnet.

"Sure! I would love to!" Kat unsnapped the strap, pulling off the helmet. She pulled the band from her hair, bent over, and flipped her gorgeous dark brown hair.

Gunner and Ratchet were at the bar cracking

open a bottle of whiskey to pour some shots as we walked in together. Fiona and Sam were at the jukebox picking out some good tunes to play. Kat hurried over to them, a huge smile planted on her adorable face. Tanya came in and hurried over to the little coven circle. She turned to me first, pointing two fingers at me, then back to herself, mouthing the words "I'm still watching you."

Skully stood beside me, his hands shoved into his pockets. "Let's go shoot a round before Gunner and Spider take over the table, Magnet."

An hour and a few beer and whiskey shots later, the clubhouse was starting to come to life. Gunner's ole lady, Fiona, picked out a few good rock songs on the jukebox. Gunner was the quiet type, like his closest brother, Ratchet. He mostly kept to himself and the club knew he battled with PTSD when he came home from Iraq. So, it was good to finally see him relax a bit more since he met the exotic dancer, Fiona. They made a good match and Gunner loved watching her dance at The Vibe, especially with that property tattoo she got inked on her ass. Now that's commitment!

I kept watch over Kat, as she fluttered around with Madge, the Prez's ole lady and the whole Coven. I tried to stay cool, playing rounds of pool with Skully, even letting Gunner kick my ass in a game too. I didn't know much about her and we couldn't really talk while on the ride. It's hard to talk while the wind is pushing you and your legs are straddled on a thundering, vibrating machine.

She rode with me, but now she was a sight for sore eyes because some of my club brothers were checking her out. We weren't together that day and it sure as hell wasn't a fucking date. Kat was standing within a circle of my brothers: Wez, Spider, Shrek, Coyote, Gambit, and the owner of Hardcore Cycles, Torque. She seemed to be enthralled by the things they were talking about. She tilted her head to one side as she drank a bottle of beer. And why the fuck was I feeling a tad bit jealous? She was focused on them, when I wanted her to focus only on me!

* * *

I had just beat Skully in our third game of pool. He started racking another set on the table, "Let's play another."

But I already cruised over to the bar. I stomped around behind it, grabbing a bottle of vodka, not concerned if Kat even drank the shit, and poured two shots. I strolled back over to the drooling pack of Chaos, maneuvering myself into the circle. She was chatting with Spider, and stopped in mid-sentence as I offered her a shot, "Here, its vodka. Share a shot with me."

She took it. I banged my glass to hers and we downed them together. Kat's eyes squeezed shut and her mouth puckered. She was bad-ass for taking the shot.

Just then, both Becky and Brandy sashayed into the clubhouse and headed right towards me. I told them both a week ago that I was taking Kat out for the Break-out ride, so there was no point in playing rock-paper-scissors to decide which one of them would ride with me. They weren't too thrilled about it either. The Coven was made-up of Madge, Tanya, Sam, Fiona, (and now Kat,) but they didn't rub elbows with my two B's. Not sure who I could blame though. My girls only came to the clubhouse to ride me, and my chopper.

I slipped my arms around both of them, as they displayed their pouty faces. "Girls, you remember Kat?"

Kat's eyes went from bright and doe-eyed, to sadness? Embarrassment? "Becky and Brandy, right?"

"So, Kat, did you enjoy riding Magnet?" Brandy just had to throw something like that in.

"She didn't ride me, babe. She rode *with* me." I had to clear that up quick.

"Yes! It was my first time on a motorcycle, so I enjoyed it very much!" Kat's adorable smile beamed.

"You work at the bookstore with Sam, right?" Becky knew that already.

"Yes, I do."

Becky giggled, "Did Magnet tell you he's really not into books? He doesn't read. Like anything. At all."

CHAPTER THREE

KAT

Just being near Magnet made my knees go weak. When I was on his chopper, my thighs hugged his hips and it made my body tingle and my nipples harden. I jumped the moment he started it and the vibrations penetrated through my jeans made me wet. I told him that it made me horny! I expected a flush of heat to crawl up my neck from embarrassment, but it didn't. And the way he smelled! I inhaled deeply every so often, just to breathe in his male scent.

Riding with Magnet and his club was so thrilling and amazing! I knew this was the chance of a lifetime and I took it! I kept wanting to pinch myself to make sure I wasn't dreaming. The minute we got back to the clubhouse, I knew the exhilarating ride was over and my heart sank. Only because I had hoped we could talk more and get to know each other. I wasn't ready to leave just yet, so I spent time with Sam and all my new friends in the Coven.

I kept looking over at Magnet playing pool with Skully. I had a small glimmer of hope that he would find me interesting. My heart skipped a beat when he came over and did a shot of vodka with me.

Magnet's lips were suddenly pressed tight when Becky said that he didn't read. He rubbed the back of his neck, "Reading takes up too much of my time, remember?"

He pulled both Becky and Brandy tighter to him, "Come on girls. Let's go do a shot for the break-out ride." Magnet turned and headed to the bar. He left me standing there with his club brothers.

Spider nodded his head toward them as they walked away, "When those girls are around, they like to smother him, Kat. I have a feeling they were a wee bit jealous that you got to ride with Magnet today, and not them." His eyes crinkled and he grinned, but my heart felt heavy.

"Oh, they can't possibly be jealous of me. Look at them! They're both gorgeous! I don't blame Magnet. The three of them look really good together. And it was nice of him to take me for a ride today." I said, as I started to leave.

"Don't go yet. Stay. You're a good friend of

ours, Kat. And the Coven loves you."

Spider cheered me up a bit. How could I say no to him? I only had eyes for Magnet, but Spider was a total hottie too, with a slender build, dark hair and a chiseled jaw. "Ok, Spider. I'll stay so that you can explain to me why Magnet's bike is called a 'shovelhead.'"

An hour later, I had finished off two more beers. I was a bit jealous of Becky and Brandy, hanging all over Magnet. That shot of vodka I shared with him plus the 2 beers had me feeling both brave and angry at the same time. I was chatting with Fiona by the juke box. Gunner stood behind her, his thumbs hooked into the belt loops of her tight jeans as she scrolled through the screen for more songs to play.

"Play something we can dance to Fiona!"

"If you say so, Kat. Let's dance!" Fiona chose a Buckcherry song: "Say Fuck It". The hard-pounding bass came through the speakers in the club. I grabbed Fiona's hand, as Gunner landed a hard smack on her ass and pulled both of us over to the group of Chaos. We bounced together to the beat of the fast rock song. Fiona slid her hands down my waist, over my hips. I bumped and grinded to the music, as the Chaos Kings began to hoot, holler and clap. I backed myself up against Spider, bending over and twerking my rear end against the front of his jeans.

"Whoa!" Spider hollered out, raising his arms.

Magnet was there. I was suddenly dizzy as he leaned down and wrapped his arm around my thighs. I was hoisted up, my stomach landing on his shoulder, and my ass up in the air. His big hand came down on my ass cheek with a loud SMACK! I heard more laughter and whistles as he carried me away from the circle of bikers.

I had to brace my hands against his broad back while I was being bounced on top of his shoulder. He was carrying me down the hall to the rooms. "What are you doing? Put me down!"

Magnet carried me through the door of a room and placed my feet back on the floor. He slowly stalked toward me. I stepped back, but the door prevented me from backing up any further. His eyes stared daggers into mine, "What the *fuck* was that all about?"

Now I was just angry, "I was just dancing with Fiona! Why do you care? This wasn't a date, right?"

"No, it wasn't. Fuck!" Magnet raked a hand through his long hair.

"So why do you care who I dance with!"

"Because my brothers were all salivating at the mouth watching you move like that!" Magnet seized my chin and his lips came crashing down on mine.

It felt just like fireworks on the fourth of July. A high-pitched moan escaped from my mouth. Magnet's hands gripped my waist, his hips slamming against mine. I felt his hardness down below as his tongue penetrated my opened lips, devouring me. My hands rose, combing through his long hair. I tilted my head so I could smash my mouth and tongue even closer to him.

He pulled away suddenly, releasing me. "No. Not doin' this."

I opened my eyes to see his brows knitted together. I suddenly felt a cold stab of rejection like a dagger into my heart. My throat felt tight. He didn't like my kiss.

I looked down at my feet, embarrassed. He grasped my chin, raising it up so I could meet his eyes again, "What I meant was yes, I wanna fuck you right here, and right now. But that would be so wrong to take advantage of you, especially after you've been drinking. You're a sweet girl, Kat."

Another opportunity I was not going to pass up! "Then take me out on a date." I smiled.

He chuckled, his voice rich and deep, "I don't date, Kitten. I just fuck."

"Well you have Becky and Brandy for that. Since you popped my cherry by taking me on my first ride, how about I pop your cherry and you take me out on a date?"

Magnet's eyes lit up and his furrowed brow disappeared. "Sure Kat. I'll take you out on a date."

My stomach fluttered because I couldn't look away from his handsome blue eyes. My heart was still pounding from the fireworks kiss we shared just moments ago.

He nodded toward the door "So, are you ready

to go back out there and suffer the hoots and hollers from my brothers? Cause right about now, they think I'm getting my fuck on with you."

He offered his hand to me and I took it, "Sure." I was certainly going to enjoy seeing the looks on Brandy and Becky's faces too.

* * *

I drove home from the clubhouse, with butterflies fluttering in my belly. I could still feel the sexual heat of Magnet's lips on mine. We exchanged numbers before I left and he told me he'd pick me up next Saturday night for that date we talked about.

I parked in front of the house and got out of my car, leaning over the driver's seat to grab my purse when I heard, "Hey Kat! Wowza! That sure is a different look for you!" I spun around to see my neighbor Stuart, sitting on his front porch with his roommates, Brett and Sean.

They lived across the street from my house. Not too long ago, I found Stuart attractive. with his

dark, messy, hair, a hipster beard, and a bad attitude. He had offered to take me out a few times, but I had to work long hours at the bookstore, plus I volunteered as a librarian aide at my local library. After being turned down so many times, Stuart finally gave up. But we remained friends along with his roommates. And after that amazing kiss from Magnet, any attraction I had for Stuart completely fizzled out.

"Is that a good thing or a bad thing, Stuart?" I hollered back to him.

"It's not bad at all! Just different," He beckoned me with a wave, "Come on over. Its Saturday night and we've got some beer."

"Nah. I'm a bit tired. Rode on a motorcycle for the very first time today!"

"That's cool! Well, have a nice night Kat."

CHAPTER FOUR

MAGNET

I knew I'd get a shitload of grief from my girls the moment I came out of the back room holding Kat's hand. So, before Brandy and Becky got *their* hands back on my ass, I exchanged numbers with her and agreed on a time for our date next weekend.

Kat tiptoed up to me and planted a kiss on my cheek, "Thanks for popping my cherry on your bike today, Magnet. It was the best experience I've ever had." Her cheeks turned a cute shade of pink. She turned away and rushed over to the Coven gals, giving out hugs and goodbyes to everyone. And then she left.

Brandy headed toward me, but her eyes stared daggers into Kat's back as she walked out to the lot. "She's cute, Magnet. But she must be a bit boring, don't you think?"

"How would you know, Brandy? You've never taken the time to talk to Kat. She's not boring. And she's a friend of the club. Don't get your thong up in a bunch, babe."

Brandy jutted out her hip, folding her arms in front of her perfectly round paid-for tits that squeezed out of the top of her tight t-shirt, "Sorry Baby. But both me and Becky were kind of feeling left out today. Let's not fight. The night is just getting started. Come play with us!"

I pulled Brandy to my chest and shoved my tongue between her glossy lips. She moaned, as I gripped both her ass cheeks and squeezed. But I kept thinking about the way Kat kissed me in that room. How sweet she tasted and how she made my heart pound fast in my chest.

"Ok babe. I'm all yours for the rest of the night."

* * *

I pulled up to the hair salon where Tanya worked. I kicked the stand down on my chopper and climbed off. Only two more days before my date with Kat and I had no fucking idea where I was going to take her! I would've asked Wez (or maybe even Skully) to give me some ideas, but I didn't want to listen to Wez busting my balls. Tanya was like a sister to me and she knew me better than most of my Chaos brothers.

I took my shades off as I entered the salon. Tanya was sitting an elderly woman underneath one of those huge blow dryers that looked like big space helmets. I sauntered over to her, getting looks from all the middle-aged female customers, as they watched my ass.

Tanya looked up from her customer in the space helmet "What's up Noah? You ok?"

I hooked the shades into my side pocket, "I need your help, sis. Let me know when you get a break so we can talk."

Tanya had that worried look, her brows all bunched up, "I'm setting Ms. Celia's hair now, so I can talk."

She stepped outside with me, her arms folded in front of her, "First things first, Noah – I watched you and Kat on the break-out ride. You did good. A true gentleman! That is, until you carried her little ass off into one of the rooms like a goddam caveman!"

"Whoa now, nothing happened. I just didn't like how she was rubbing up all over Spider, that's all!"

"Ok. Well. That's all I wanted to say about it. But you did good. Kat is usually quiet and reserved. She's like Sam. Seeing her face all lit up and glowing was a good thing."

"Well that's what I need to talk to you about.

I'm taking Kat out on a date this Saturday."

Tanya's brows lifted. "A date? Do you even *know* what that is?"

I grunted "Yes damn it! But I've never been on one."

"Never?"

"Never!"

Tanya began to laugh at me.

"Ok. Go ahead and laugh all you want. It was never about dating with me. It's all about fuckin, remember?"

"Oh, Noah." She stepped up to me, poking her finger into my chest. "Well, where ever you take Kat for your first date, you'd better not take advantage of the situation, just to get down her pants!"

"I won't, sis. I promise. So, tell me: what did you and Skully do on your first date?"

"He took me for a ride on his Superglide, and we stopped in at a coffee shop to chat. It was really nice." She looked away, reminiscing.

"Well, Kat *did* enjoy the ride I gave her last weekend. I'll take her out on the bike again. She was diggin' the loud pipes when I revved my throttle a few times." Then the idea came to me, like a light bulb switching on over my head.

I grabbed Tanya, smacking a kiss on her cheek. "Thanks, Tanya. I knew I could talk to you. Wez and the other brothers would've just busted my balls all day."

CHAPTER FIVE

KAT

I had the jitters. I was pacing back and forth in front of the living room window, waiting for Magnet to pull up on his chopper. I looked down at myself and contemplated whether or not I should change into something different. Magnet had texted me the day before and told me to wear jeans and boots because he planned on taking me out for a ride again.

"You look fine, Katrina. Stop fidgeting or you're going to wear out that carpet." Mom teased me from the kitchen.

The loud "blap-blap" sound of Magnet's pipes

came to my ears even before he turned the corner onto our street. I exhaled, not realizing I held my breath as he rolled up in front of the house and planted his boots down. Before he turned the bike off, he revved the throttle a few times, making my nipples harden instantly.

"Don't go out there Kat! Make him come to the door and greet us. I want to take a look at him myself!" Mom was already heading to the door.

The doorbell rang, and mom opened it as I stood behind her. I squeezed my thighs together, holding back a groan at the sight of Magnet. He was sex on a stick!

His hair was tied back, and his huge body leaned against the door frame. He slid his shades down the bridge of his nose, displaying a handsome grin. "Hello, you must be Kat's mother," He offered his hand. My mom's mouth hung open, and I hoped a fly wouldn't land in it. She took his huge hand in hers, "Yes, I'm Jean. Pleasure to meet you. Uh…Magnet, right?"

"Yes ma'am. That's what I go by."

Once my mom released Magnet's hand I stepped around her, pulled her to me and kissed her cheek, "I won't be out too late Mom. Love you!"

"You two have fun, just please be careful with her on that bike, Magnet!" Mom called out as I grabbed his hand, and we rushed down my front steps to his bike.

My mom watched us from the front door as he

put the extra helmet on my head and snapped it under my chin, just like he did last week. I was feeling giddy, like I could float up to the clouds, knowing I would be so close to Magnet again. He climbed on first, then I did and he started up the chopper. It roared back to life. I looked at my mom. She jumped, and brought her hand up to her chest.

I anchored my boots on the pegs, and wrapped my arms around him, pressing my hands into his hard stomach, my chin on his shoulder, "So where are you taking me on our date?"

He pivoted his head toward me. I couldn't resist and kissed him on his cheek. He smirked, "Just hold on tight Kitten. It's a surprise I guarantee you're going to like!"

Magnet twisted the throttle and we rolled away from my house and out of my neighborhood.

* * *

After an hour of riding down back roads and the interstate highway, Magnet planted his boots down at a park in Washington DC. As I looked around, I saw picnic tables and green grass. We were right next to the Potomac River. I heard the thundering roar and felt vibrations through my entire body before I saw it. I looked up at the sky – a massive airplane flew right over us, landing hundreds of yards away at the Washington National Airport.

My mouth dropped open. I was frozen right

there on Magnet's bike; my arms were still wrapped around him. He turned to me, "Like that, Kat? "

I shut my mouth, and grinned as another loud thunderous sound boomed in our ears – Another airplane in the sky was beginning its decent, "I fucking love it!"

He chuckled "Climb off kitten. Let's go sit at one of those picnic tables and watch those massive beasts land and take off."

After we climbed off his bike, he pulled a small flask out of a little black bag that hung in between the handlebars. There was no one else at the park but us. We sat together on the wooden picnic table on a flat grassy area.

Magnet twisted the little cap off his flask and offered it to me. "Here take a shot."

I took a sip and coughed, "Wow!"

He chuckled as I handed it back to him, and tossed it back for a swig, "You're a little wildcat, aren't you? You didn't even ask me what it is!"

I smiled and batted my eyes "I can be." His head fell back and he laughed, his deep rich voice making my nipples harden yet again. "I really like your laugh, Magnet."

"Thanks kitten."

The sun was setting as another plane flew over us. Nothing else was said and we both felt nervous. Maybe because it was the first time we had a moment alone to actually talk to each other. And since this was Magnet's first date, I took the opportunity to learn as much as I could about him.

"I know your brothers call you Magnet, but what's your real name?'

"Noah. Noah Davenport. That's my real name."

"Noah. I like it. So, tell me a little bit about yourself Noah. Where did you grow up? Where did you go to school?"

"Well, I grew up in the same neighborhood as Tanya. I'm the only kid and my parents are still married and still live in the house I grew up in."

"You and Tanya grew up together?"

"Yep. Tanya lived across the street from me. When we were in grade school, she'd be outside playing with those Barbie and Ken dolls with other girls her age. She had really long hair and wore it up in a ponytail all the time. Me and the boys I hung out with used to pass the football around out on the street. One day, my buddy dared me to go and pull Tanya's ponytail. Of course, I had to prove to my friends that I'd take any dare. But I only pulled her ponytail once. And never again."

"Oh no…"

"She threw her Barbie and Ken dolls down in the grass, and chased my ass! My buddies all laughed. Her friends cheered her on, hoping she'd catch me. Well she did."

"What did she do?"

"She kneed me right in the balls! I went down on the first count, holding onto them, hoping they wouldn't fall off! Fuckin hurt like a son of a bitch!"

I couldn't help but giggle and snort.

"Yeah, yeah. Well I survived the knee strike to my balls and we've been close friends ever since. Tanya even started throwing the football with us boys. Her girlfriends would roll their eyes at her. She was a bit of a tomboy and I think she just played Barbies with the girls so she would fit in with them. But she fit in better with us boys. "

"But when we both got to high school, Tanya was all filled out and drop-dead gorgeous. I only felt sister love for her, but I had a few scraps with some of the guys, fending them off. She wasn't interested in them. She was more about grades and other things I guess."

"Tanya loves you, Noah. I can see it. You two still kid around just like brother and sister. You're both lucky to have that kind of relationship."

"Yeah. She's always been there for me. And I've always been there for her, until she met Skully, or Owen. I didn't like him at first, none of Chaos did. But he proved himself to both Tanya and to the club. That's why he's a member now. He's a good guy. And everyone loves his son, Jake."

"Did you like high school?"

He shrugged his broad shoulders. "Eh, it was ok I guess. I played senior varsity football. I was a tight-end"

I bet he was…

"I was pretty good at playing football. But it

was just for fun, to get through high school. I dropped out my senior year and started at the bottom, working with my dad doing manual labor. He's a contractor for a home building business in the area. My parents are pretty well off. I like working for him. And I make good money too. I own a townhouse a few miles from the clubhouse."

"So that's how you keep your body so…. So…. Nice." I couldn't help myself.

He chuckled, "Well I do work out at the gym, too. Plus, I help out part-time with some of the older women who come in to learn how to use the workout machines. They like to flirt with me, and I let them. Maybe I inspire them to take better care of themselves and feel young again."

"Oh, I bet you do, Noah. That's really sweet. Most guys your age want to work out with other guys or gals their same age."

"Ok, enough about me. Tell me about you Kat. Or is it Katrina?"

"Yes, its Katrina. You met my mother tonight."

"And she's gorgeous, like her daughter." His deep voice made my toes curl inside my boots.

"Thank you, Noah. She's my rock. My hero. My dad skipped town when I was only 5 years old. Not sure where he lives or if he's even alive. So, my mom took care of both of us. She met Frank when I was a teenager and I have a step-sister, Lillian. We have nothing in common, but we are as civil as stepsisters can be I guess. Well Frank died a few years ago of a heart attack. We were all devastated. He was a good man and loved us both. I still live with my mom. She's the best roommate ever."

"That's great, Kat. I know a lot of women who can't be in the same room with their mothers, or their sisters. You and your mom are lucky to have each other. So, I take it you like to read books?"

"Oh yes, do I ever!"

"Like what kind?"

"Oh, let's see. I love to read fantasy, horror, romance, sci-fi, even memoirs and biographies, self-help books…"

Magnet began to rub the back of his neck; his eyes weren't focused on me anymore and he just stared off into space. "I'm sorry Noah. I know that all sounds so damn boring."

He shook his head and looked down at the grass. "No. It's not boring at all, Kat. It's just…well, Becky was right when she told you that I don't read. Anything. It's because I can't."

I felt a heaviness in my chest. Sadness. He was embarrassed!

He was still looking at the grass and he leaned his head back to watch another massive thundering airplane fly past us. I reached over, placing my fingertips to his scruffy bearded cheek and turned him to look at me, "Noah. It's ok. Just because you can't read doesn't make you less attractive. Not to me. You are so very handsome. And you're a good man."

Magnet pulled me to him and claimed my lips. I grabbed his broad shoulders, my nails digging into them, clinging to him as his tongue plundered and explored my mouth. He growled then, his lips pulling away. He planted soft kisses across my jaw and down my neck. My breath hitched when his hand meandered up my top. I cried out as he pinched and rolled my beaded nipple between his finger and thumb. My bra was a hinderance and his relentless teasing of my nipple made me arch my back, needing more of his touch.

"Don't stop Noah, please! I need more!"

His lips left my neck and he looked at me, his blue eyes full of yearning fire. For me. "You do something to me Kat. I've never felt like I could be myself and let go. Like I can be when I'm with you." The side of his mouth lifted "My dick has never been this hard for a woman, and believe me, I've been with a lot of women. Just sitting here, talking with you. It's a fucking turn on!"

He dipped down again and his mouth latched onto the same nipple he just tormented with his finger and thumb. I sucked in another breath, and my jaw hung open, his mouth sending lightning bolts of pleasure throughout my body and settling between my thighs. My hand's natural reflex reached down and grasped the front of his jeans, feeling his enormous and erect maleness that was all Noah.

He pulled away and I suddenly felt alone. I

opened my eyes to see his furrowed brow, "I shouldn't have pushed you like this," he pressed his palms down along the tops of his thighs. I could see how hard he was for me. "I didn't take you out today just to fuck you, Kat."

"I know that, Noah." But I was hoping he would.

He jumped off the picnic table and offered his hand to me. "It's getting dark. And I don't want us riding on the highway too late at night. I'll take you home."

CHAPTER SIX

MAGNET

Kat was quiet as a mouse behind me as I rode back to her house. Thank goodness my dick settled down because it took all my willpower not to pull over somewhere secluded and rip her shirt off to squeeze, lick, and suck on those luscious tits of hers! But that would have led me to getting her completely naked and ramming my hard cock balls deep inside her. And if I did that to her, I wouldn't be able to forgive myself.

I walked Kat up to her door, like a gentleman is supposed to do on a date. I gave her an innocent kiss on her soft lips (no tongue). That's when she jumped up, wrapped her arms around my neck and thrusted her tongue into my mouth! My dick slammed up against my zipper as I pulled her closer, her tits crushing against my chest.

I pulled away, "OK, little wildcat. Get on inside."

Her eyes were sad, even though she smiled at me, "Thank you Noah. I had a wonderful time with you tonight. If you ever want to practice your dating skills, I hope you'll ask me out again sometime soon."

I chuckled "Thanks Kat. I had a great time too. I just might take you up on that offer."
* * *

I had my throttle wide open as I left Kat's house and sped my way to the clubhouse with a raging hard on. There were only a few bikes parked in the lot as I pulled in next to Wez's softail, painted flat black, with the word 'HARDCORE' emblazoned on both sides of the tank.

Wez was at the pool table, playing a lonely game with himself. He rose up from his last unsuccessful shot, "Play a round with me Magnet. Hell, no one else will. I really suck at this."

"Yeah brother. Rack 'em. I need a stiff shot of whatever the fuck is behind that bar first." I ambled up as Spider and Coyote were sitting on stools, cigarette smoke floating around them.

I went around the bar, grabbing the painted skull full of KAH Tequila and poured myself a shot.

"Having a bad day brother?" Coyote asked. I

almost felt like busting his jaw at that moment, just because his eyes were focused on Kat's tits the weekend before.

Then I was just angry at myself. Coyote was my brother. He was a scrapper. But he never started a fight, he just ended it with his quick moves and jabs. "Eh, yeah. Went on a fuckin date tonight."

Spider's brows went up "A date? Do you even know what that is?"

"Yes!" It was like de ja vu. Tanya had said the exact same thing earlier.

Spider chuckled "Just bustin' your balls, brother. It couldn't have been all that fuckin bad. And I'm guessing it wasn't with Becky or Brandy."

"Nope. I took Kat out."

"Bring that skull over here, man. Let's do this!" Wez called me over to the pool table.

I came over and handed him the skull and shot glass, then went around the other side and took a shot to break. Wez poured, leaning his head back and guzzled the shot. He imitated the Jack Nicholson move from "Easy Rider", cranking his elbow against his ribs and shouting "Nit-Nit-Nit!" as the balls knocked against each other, scattering across the table.

"Thought you'd still be at the kink club tonight, Wez."

The King of kink was not only a Chaos King club member, he was also a member of a BDSM club called The Underground. "Well that was the plan,

Stan. But I just wasn't feeling it tonight."

An hour later I had way too may KAH shots to count, and began to see 30 balls on the table instead of the standard 15. I saw double of everything around me as I staggered and stumbled back to the bar with Wez. We were both shit-faced.

"I'm proud of you brother. Not only did you take that nice girl out on a date, you're showing your B's who calls the shots." Wez was slurring now.

Things were spinning. My chin fell to my chest. "Well, I didn't tell Becky or Brandy I was taking Kat out. They weren't too thrilled last weekend when she rode with me."

Wez slapped me on the back, "Well what they don't know won't hurt 'em. We'll just keep it on the DL."

"What's on the DL?" we both turned to see Becky and Brandy standing right behind us.

Wez wobbled a few steps up to Becky "Nothing to worry your pretty little head about. You need to learn some rules around here, darlin'. When the brothers are conversing, you need to show a little respect and mind your own fuckin' business." He turned and staggered away.

I saw two Becky's and two Brandy's. One of them wrapped their arms around me "Are you drunk already baby?" she crooned in my ear.

"I'm ok. Just got the party started early tonight, that's all."

And that's the last thing I remember saying,

because I was pulled off my stool by both girls and stumbled with them down the hall to one of the rooms. The door shut and one of them sat on her knees in, front of me, fumbling with my zipper. My iron-hard cock penetrated her warm, wet mouth. The other one stood beside me as she shoved her tongue in my mouth. I reached up, grabbing her round solid tit. It wasn't soft and squeezable like Kat's.

My cock slipped out of her mouth as I stepped back from both of them. "Not into it tonight girls. Gonna crash." I stumbled to a bed, falling down face first. And I was out for the count.

* * *

I didn't want to open my eyes. My head felt like it was being squeezed between a fucking vice. My mouth was parched and my gut felt queasy. I sat up and almost wretched, tasting bile with the mix of that demonic tequila I drank the night before. I opened one eye, and my swimmy brain realized that I wasn't in my bed. I was in one of the beds at the clubhouse, alone. My jeans and boxers were bunched around my upper thighs.

Then I remembered Becky sucking my cock the night before. Or was that Brandy? It didn't matter. I passed out on both of them. I knew they would have their claws out the next time I saw them, which would be in the next day or two. I guess I deserved it. I took Kat out on an actual date, then grabbed and pawed at her like some perverted asshole trying to get my fuck on. When I took her home, I rode straight to the clubhouse to fuck my girls with Mr. Limp Tequila Dick!

Yeah, you're the fuckin' Chick Magnet, Noah. I knew I had to make it up to Becky and Brandy. I had nothing in common with Kat, other than wanting to get down her pants and sink my dick in her balls deep. That was all I was good for anyway, and I was sure Kat wanted a man with more brain cells than I would ever have.

CHAPTER SEVEN

KAT

My mom set the bag of charcoal down on a picnic table, "So Noah is coming too, right?"

"Yes, Mom. He'll be coming to the cookout with Ratchet - I mean James - and Sam, too."

"Good. They are your friends Kat. And you invite friends to cookouts."

It wasn't exactly *our* cookout, but rather a neighborhood community cookout that was held every spring and summer. Neighbors gathered with their friends and family at the community club house and pool. Picnic tables in rows sat under a huge pavilion next to a pool full of kids splashing around.

Two weeks had passed since I went on that incredible date with Noah, but we hadn't spoken or texted each other since. I moped around at work and at home. My mom tried to cheer me up by telling me that Magnet respected me and wanted to get to know me better before getting too intimate, which, she said, was rare for most men my age. I loved her so much. She would always say nice things to comfort me. But my chest still hurt. Magnet put out so much sexy charisma standing next to me, a plain-looking book nerd with zero sex appeal. Why would he bother wanting me when he had his two biker chick beauties, Becky and Brandy?

Just then, Lillian pulled up and climbed out of her nice brand-new Lexus, wearing a turquoise blue form-fitting dress and wedge sandals. All of the men in the vicinity immediately noticed her.

She came up and gave me the usual kiss on both cheeks, "Hi Kat!" She stepped back to inspect my attire, which was a bit different than what she usually saw me wear, "Wow Kat! Those are some *really* short shorts you're wearing today! You actually look better in your long flowy dresses and skirts."

Did I detect a hint of jealousy? I smiled at her, but my eyes didn't, "Well it *is* summer and sometimes a girl just needs to accentuate her attributes. Right Mom?"

Mom started working her charcoal grill, and turned to us, "That's right, Katrina. And you have so many attributes to show off." She winked.

Just then, the rumbling of pipes came to everyone's ears as James and Noah rolled into the parking lot on their motorcycles. Sam sat on Ratchet's black night train, leaning on the backrest, looking like a sexy biker beauty. I walked over to them as they parked, my eyes drinking in the sight of Noah. His hair was tied back under his helmet, as his muscular body sat stretched out on his yellow chopper. His beard had grown out some too, making him look more like a barbaric Viking!

Ratchet and Sam climbed of their bike, as Noah was shutting his off. He slid is glasses down his nose, like he did when he met my Mom, and his eyes roamed down my body, from my yellow tank top to my white cut-off shorts. My heart skipped a beat, knowing that he liked what he was checking out!

I squeezed Sam, whispering next to her ear, "Thank you for coming, Sam. I'm so happy James came! And Noah too, of course!" Ratchet went around to the back of his bike to pull some things out of the bag that was strapped to the backrest.

"You going to greet me with a nice hug like that too, kitten?" Noah was off his bike, his brawny arms opened wide.

My knees felt weak, but I managed to step into his embrace, "Hi Noah. Thank you for coming."

"Thanks for inviting me, Kat." He leaned away, but still kept his arms wrapped around me, "How've you been? Good?"

I leaned my head back, "Yes, thanks. And you?"

He smiled, "Can't complain. It's really good to see you again. Sam made some jello shooters we can share with your neighbor friends today."

The delicious smells of hotdogs, hamburgers, and smoldering charcoal wafted around the pavilion as music played from someone's wireless speaker. Both Sam and James - and now Noah - had met my mom before. After giving her hugs, Sam handed her some colorful little containers of jello shooters.

I had two of them myself and was feeling giddy. I saw the look on Lillian's face when she saw me walk toward the pavilion with Noah's well-built arm wrapped around my waist, walking in stride with me. Lillian's jaw dropped open, her eyes round as saucers. I really shocked her that day – wearing sexy cut off short shorts and walking with the hottest man at the cookout.

Lillian scooted in next to me and Sam. We were talking, giggling and doing another jello shooter together. Sam held a blue one out to Lillian, "Would you like one? Its vodka."

Lillian held her hand up, smiling at Sam, "Ah. No thank you." She leaned into me with a hushed voice, "Noah is kind of brutish, isn't he?" She giggled, "I bet he's as sharp as a bowling ball…"

That was it. I was done with Lillian, and after a few jello shooters, my mouth seemed to lose its filter, "I think you're jealous, Lillian!"

"Oh Katrina, I sure as hell am not!"

"Yes, you are. You're jealous because for once, the most handsome man within a hundred yards of both of us is more attracted to me than you!"

"Don't be such a bitch Kat," Lillian turned away from us, but I stepped up to her, "I'm not finished. You could be a super-genius, with a high IQ, a great body and fashion model looks, but if you're ugly on the inside - it shows on the outside. And people see that. Because all this," I gestured toward her nice petite figure, "fades with age someday. But the beauty inside will always shine through. Will *your* beauty shine someday Lillian?"

Her eyes became round saucers, and her nostrils flared as she strutted away from both of us.

"Whoa Kat, that was kick-ass! Your cat claws came out!" Sam said, watching Lillian walk away. Then we both busted out laughing.

"What was all that about, Rabbit?" James' deep rumbly voice interrupted us.

We spun around to see both James and Noah. Sam winked at James "Oh nothing, James. Lillian just hates jello-shooters."

* * *

The sun was setting behind the summer green trees as everyone packed up food, kids' toys, and grills. James and Sam climbed back on their bike as Noah wrapped his arms around me. He brushed my lips with a soft kiss. "I had a great time with you, Kat. And I'm taking you up on your offer. Let's go out on another one of those dates."

My heart skipped a beat, "Yes Noah. I would love that."

Ratchet's biked roared to life and he revved the throttle. Noah climbed on his bike, strapped on his helmet, put on his shades and they rolled out together. Their loud pipes could be heard several blocks away as they left my neighborhood.

"Hey, Kat! Some cool friends you got there." Stuart walked with me back to the pavilion to help pack up things.

"Yes, they are a lot of fun. Good people."

Stuart raked a hand through his dark hair. "Does your bookstore still take in used ones? Cause I have a box full at the house." He had that boyish charm like Noah, but instead of the bold biker vibe that Noah gave off, Stuart was more the hipster-type with a laidback attitude, and a long dark beard growing down to his upper chest.

"Yes, we do Stuart! You can bring them by the store and I'll give you a credit for the trade."

"Well I'm flying out on business Monday. You wanna just come over now and check them out? Take them to the store for me? I don't need a credit slip."

"Sure Stuart, thanks. That's really nice of you."

I hopped into Stuart's SUV, letting my mom know I was going to grab the box of books from his house. Since he just lived across the street from me, I figured he could carry it back for me.

The possibly of feeling any threat from Stuart never came to me because I always thought of him as a friend. He opened his front door and pointed to his room at the end of the hall. And I didn't think anything of it as I walked into his room. But the moment I realized that Brett and Sean were still at the cook-out and we were alone, it was too late.

I walked up to his dresser, where the box of books sat, pulling a few out, when I heard Stuart's footsteps behind me and the sound of the door shutting.

I spun around but it was too late. Stuart seized me by my arms and tossed me onto his bed. He landed on top of me, pinning my arms down over my head.

"Get off me Stuart!" I screamed at him, my eyes wide with fear and shock.

His fiery eyes glared back at me, his breathing heavy, his nostrils flaring, "Is that biker your boyfriend Kat?"

I bucked my hips as hard as I could, but Stuart was bigger and heavier than me, "That's none of your fucking business!" Everything was happening too fast. My heart rate was at full speed. I was trapped!

"I know you fucked him! You're a biker whore! You're gonna fuck me too!"

He kept both my arms pinned above me with just one hand as his other roughly fumbled with my button and zipper on my shorts. I screamed at the top of my lungs. He rose up and back handed me, right across the cheek. I shut my eyes tight, seeing stars behind my eyelids as he continued to assault me. I screamed again as he thrusted his fingers deep inside me.

"Shut up Kat. I know you like this!" His growl was terrifying.

A split-second opportunity gave me the luck I needed. Stuart loosened his grip on my arms, while he continued assaulting me with his fingers. I broke free, pushing against his chest. His hand came out of my shorts. I hiked my knee up, striking him hard between his legs. He fell back, landing on the floor and curled up hugging his crotch.

I was off the bed in seconds and wrenching the door open. I ran as fast as I could across the street to my house.

CHAPTER EIGHT

MAGNET

Both Ratchet and I were twisting the caps back onto our gas tanks at the station when I heard my phone buzzing in my bag. I pulled it out and hit the talk button instantly as soon I saw Kat's name glowing on my screen.

"Hey kitten – "

"Noah, It's her mom, Jean…" The hair on the back of my neck stood up when I heard Kat crying in the background.

"What's wrong with Kat? Is she hurt?"

"No. Well, yes. But she's ok now. Our neighbor attacked her Noah!"

"I'll be there in ten minutes, Jean."

"Ok, please hurry Noah" Jean's voice cracked as I hung up with her.

I climbed back on my bike and hollered over to Ratchet and Sam as I started it back up, "We gotta go back to Kat's house. Some soon-to-be-dead motherfucker hurt Kat!"

"Let's roll brother", Ratchet and Sam rode out of the station with me, our throttles twisted wide open.

I gritted my teeth so hard my jaw hurt, "MOTHER FUCKER!" I roared, as bits gravel flew off my back tire.

* * *

We pulled up eight minutes later. My whole body was tense as I climbed off the bike and headed up the stairs to the front door. Ratchet and Sam were close behind. I knocked three times and Jean appeared. Dried tears down her cheeks, her eyes puffy. She stepped back to allow us to come in.

Kat was sitting on the couch. She vaulted off it, landing smack dab on me, her arms came around my neck. She was trembling and began to sob.

I covered her little body with my arms, burying my face into the crook of her neck. "It's ok Kat. You're safe now." I had to choke back the painful lump that rose up my throat.

I lifted her chin to look into her eyes. I saw a

red blemish, the size of my palm, that covered her right cheek.

"I never thought he would ever do something like that! I was stupid to go into his house alone. Maybe I led him on. Or maybe I made him angry because I blew him off when he'd ask me out – "

"No. Don't say that. You are not stupid. He took advantage of an opportunity to hurt you. And I guarantee he's done this to other women before you, Kat. How did you get away from that piece of shit?"

"I did what Tanya did to you! I kneed him as hard as I could. Right in his balls."

I could have laughed at that moment, but smiled down at her instead, "My brave kitten…" I looked over at Sam, "Stay with Kat and Jean."

Kat clung tightly to Sam. Ratchet was a right behind me as we ambled up to Stuart's house. He walked out the front door, and I threw a swift hook to his jaw, my knuckles slamming against his cheek bone. He dropped to the deck, landing hard on his ass.

"Not done with you yet. Get up motherfucker!"

Everything blacked out around me. I saw only tunnel vision. I was aware that two other guys were on that deck too. But I knew that Ratchet had my back, and all it would take is one look from him, and those boys would be pissin' in their pants.

Stuart's shorts probably smelled like shit as he scooted away from me, holding his jaw, "Sorry man!

It won't happen again!"

I was on him then, fisting his shirt, my face an inch away from his, "You got that right you piece of shit! If you ever touch Kat, or even *look* at her, I'll come back and cut your dick and balls off, and shove 'em down your fucking throat!"

I shoved off him, making my way back to Kat's house. I heard Ratchet before he turned to follow me, "If we even get a *whiff* of a rumor that any of you motherfuckers hurt a woman? Your body parts will be my trophies."

* * *

Kat wanted me to stay with her. Ratchet and Sam left as I held her on the couch. Jean sat with us too, putting a cold towel on Kat's cheek. Kat sobbed and shook as I held her tight. I didn't know any other way to comfort her, but I guess it helped because she was fast asleep soon after. Her steady breathing tickled the side of my neck, as her quiet little snores were music to my ears.

It was dark out when Kat stirred and whimpered. She opened her puffy eyes and smiled at me, "Noah."

I smiled down at her, "you have the cutest little snore."

She gasped "I snore?"

"Yep, you sure do kitten. And I love it."

CHAPTER NINE

KAT

I wouldn't have been able to keep myself together if it hadn't been for the support from my mom, James, Sam, and of course, Noah. We watched from the front door as Noah punched Stuart, knocking him on his ass. And James was right there with him. The hell that Sam had been living with the Hell Hounds MC almost did her in. But James, the protective alpha caveman was her salvation. I can only imagine how much rage was boiling up inside of him after hearing what Stuart had done to me.

It made me feel protected and vindicated when Noah slammed his fist into Stuart's face, causing him to scurry away like a wounded animal.

Sam was my rock. I clung to her, hoping the strength she possessed would rub off on me. She told me that I was one of the bravest women she knew and what Stuart did to me was not my fault. That he deserved far worse than what Noah just fed him.

I've never felt as safe and protected as I did when Noah held me in his strong arms. I cried myself to sleep on the couch and dreamt of Noah. He was sitting on a park bench with a beautiful lioness lying at his feet. A kitten sat in his lap, its little paws and teeth pulling on his long hair. And he laughed, his rich voice giving me tingles on my nipples and between my thighs. The lioness roared.

I woke up and there he was, holding me close to his big warm body. I took a hot shower, steaming up my bathroom as I scrubbed every inch of my body vigorously, trying to get the touch of Stuart off me. Later, Noah sat on the edge of my bed and tucked me in.

He looked sad and angry. "It's my fault, Kat. I should have stayed with you and your mom after the cookout. Then this wouldn't have happened."

I rose up and touched his bearded cheek. "No, Noah. It's not your fault. If Stuart hadn't hurt me today, he would have tried some other day. I wanted you to hit him. I wanted you to scare him. He won't ever do that again. Thank you."

"I'll support you if you want to go to the law.

Get charges pressed against him. He'll have a rap sheet that'll fuck up his career and everything else in his life."

"No. What you did to him was enough justice for me. I will never be afraid to look him in the eyes again."

Noah leaned in and brushed a soft kiss on my lips. "You're part of the Chaos Coven. You're part of my tribe. I care about you, Kat."

I swallowed, to hold back tears. I laid back down and he pulled the covers over me, "Get some sleep, kitten. I'll call you in the morning."

"Promise?"

"I promise."

* * *

Noah kept his promise and called me early the next morning as I got dressed for work to open the bookstore. I was meeting with William, the owner and manager. Will had always been good to both me and Sam, giving us time off when we needed it and letting us pick out any books that we liked to take them home and read. I felt a little anxious and jumpy after everything that happened the day before and was a bit nervous to meet with Will.

"Don't be nervous. Maybe he's giving you a raise, Kat. You're tons smarter than me – "

"Stop that, Noah. You're a smart man. And a good man."

"Yeah, Yeah. Well if you knew what I was thinking right about now, you'd take back the good man part."

I giggled and squeezed my thighs together at hearing Noah's deep voice over the phone. "Yeah? So, what were you just thinking about, Chick Magnet?"

"I was thinkin' about those magnificent tits of yours. And how they hardened to little pebbles when I pinched and pulled them that night on the park bench. You got my dick rock hard…"

I looked down at my chest, "They're not all that, Noah."

"Yes, they are Kat. They're fucking perfect!"

I giggled some more, feeling very sexy at that moment. The things he said to me, and how he touched me, made me feel that way. "Who knows? Maybe I'll let you get to third base next time you take me out on a date!" I sounded so different - my naughty side was coming out!

"Fuck yeah! What are you doing tonight after work?"

* * *

I felt more at ease after talking with Noah as I drove to work that morning. Will was already at the bookstore, sitting in the back office. It was small, with a desk, a computer, with boxes of used books piled alongside one wall. Will was a sweet man in his late fifties. He opened the bookstore back in the early 1980's. He sat at the desk, wearing his glasses and squinted at the old computer screen.

I came in and sat in a chair across from him, "HI, Will. Why don't you invest a little money and buy a more up-to-date PC, with a bigger monitor?"

"Hi, Kat." His chin came down, and his eyes came above his glasses, "Well that's what I want to talk to you about."

"Oh yeah? Is everything ok?"

"Yes. Everything is fine. But I've been thinking lately about the future. I'm not getting any younger. My two daughters are grown and have left home, so now it's just me and the wife. We want to spend some quality one-on-one time together, like we did when we were younger. So, I'm promoting you to manager."

"What?"

Will chuckled, "You heard me Kat. I want you to manage my bookstore. Sam has been here about a year now. You two together have done a great job of keep everything in working order. I trust the both of you to run this business. And I'll be raising your pay of course."

Will stood up from the desk, and leaned over it to offer me his hand, "Will you accept the position Kat?"

I jumped out of the chair, almost knocking it over behind me. I took his hand and shook it, "Yes Will, I accept! Thank you so much for this opportunity!" My heart was soaring!

* * *

Noah pulled up in front of my house later that afternoon, but instead of riding his chopper, he drove his truck.

"Don't run, Kat!" Mom called out as I raced down my front steps later and leapt into Noah's arms just moments after he got out of the truck.

He lifted me off my feet as I wrapped my arms around his neck, "Not only did I get a raise - I also got promoted to Manager!"

Noah's head fell back and he chuckled, squeezing me, "I knew it Kat! Congrats! We'll need to celebrate!" He put me back down, "But tonight I'm taking you to the drive-in."

"What's a drive-in?"

"You don't know what that is? You park in this wide-open gravel car lot and hang this old clunky piece of metal on your car window for sound and watch a movie on a big fucking movie screen. They even have a snack bar and swing sets for kids. Like in that chick flick, 'Grease'. "

I jumped, "Oh that sounds like so much fun! Is that why you told me I didn't have to wear jeans today since we're not riding your bike?"

"Yeah Kitten," His big hands moved down to my ass and squeezed, "And I like seeing you in your summer dresses. It's sexy as fuck!"

"...and it would be easy-access for him to get *under* my dress," I thought to myself.

Noah drove us out west near the Shenandoah Mountains and parked in the gravel lot next to a metal box speaker that hung from a pole. A line of cars and trucks pulled in and parked as well, and people brought out lawn chairs and sat in truck beds. Some kids were in their pajamas, with pillows and blankets. It was dusk now, and the sun was lowering on the horizon behind while lightening bugs began to appear near the swing sets in front of the movie screen.

A large cupholder console in the middle of Noah's truck divided us, making me feel like I was so far away from him. He put the truck in park and shut off his engine.

He turned to me, placing his elbow on the steering wheel, "So, this is a drive-in theater. They're almost extinct these days. I remember my parents taking me here when I was a kid. My dad let me sit in the bed of his truck with a lawn chair. He'd buy me all the food I wanted, and I'd get so stuffed on hotdogs, soda and candy, I thought I'd pop like a tick!"

I laughed at that, picturing Noah as a boy, shoving hotdogs and candy in his mouth, dressed in his pajamas.

"By the time the movie started, I would doze off. And I'm sure that gave my parents some alone time inside the truck to do what couples do at drive-ins - they made out!"

"That sounds so romantic Noah. It's nice to have fond memories like that as a child."

"Well, I can't complain. My parents were good to me. And I'm grateful for that. I know lots of people who didn't have it as good as me growing up."

Noah combed a hand through his long hair. Then he said, "Hey Kat…I was wondering if you could help me with something."

I leaned over closer to him, "Sure Noah, If I can, I will."

"Well, you know that I can't read very good. My club brothers don't know anything about it. Tanya does though. I know that someday soon, my dad is going to need me to step up and help with his home building business. I cruised along all these years working for my dad since I quit high school. I want to hire a tutor. To teach me to read. Then go and get my GED. And I'll probably need your help to fill out any paperwork."

Warmth spread my body, "That's a brilliant idea! And I will help you in any way you need it, Noah."

He leaned down, pulling a lever and shoved his seat back, "Enough talking for now kitten. Climb over here and plant that cute ass on my lap."

He didn't have to say that twice! I climbed over the console and did exactly that! He was hard already, and I wiggled my rear. He bucked his hips. "Yeah, baby. I'm taking you to first base."

Movie trailers appeared on the billboard movie

screen and the metal speaker came alive with music as our mouths joined roughly, tasting each other. My hands meandered up into his long hair. His roamed from my calf, to my knees and underneath my long dress.

I broke the kiss, panting, "Please Noah. Touch me." I begged.

"Touch you Kitten? Where?"

"Touch my pussy. Please."

"Fuck..." he groaned as his fingers yanked aside my panties, and one slid deep inside me.

I cried out, feeling an orgasm already rising inside me.

"Dammit, Kat. Your pussy is slippery wet and so tight!"

My head fell back, and Noah's mouth claimed my neck, devouring my skin with his tongue, lips and teeth. His hips rose, pressing roughly against my ass, as his finger glided in and out of my wet center. His thumb tormented my clit, rubbing it softly.

"You're going to make me come!"

"Yes, I am, Kitten."

I cried out his name and climaxed suddenly, a jolt of hot erotic pleasure spreading throughout my body.

My breath came out in pants as my climax ended. I pressed my cheek against Noah's chest and wrapped my arms around his neck. His heart pounded just as fast and I heard him mumble, "You're so beautiful, Kat."

I leaned away to look into his eyes full of sexual need, "I love you Noah." I couldn't have stopped myself from saying it. It's what I had felt ever since he caught me in his arms that day at the bookstore.

He smiled and pressed me back into his chest. "I know."

CHAPTER TEN

MAGNET

I was such a god damn prick when Kat told me she loved me that night at the drive-in. She totally caught me off-guard when she said those three little words. Yeah, I loved my parents, and my club. But I'd never felt love for a woman in my entire life, and no woman had ever said that to me before.

It may have just been in the heat of the moment as she exploded with an orgasm, as I played with her sweet little pussy. I was a piece of shit for touching her like that, especially after what happened to her just the day before when Stuart hurt her.

That was two weeks ago, but we talked on the phone every day since. I just had to hear her voice every day since we were both busy working and she even more now with her new manager job at the bookstore.

I sat at my kitchen table, staring at the paperwork I needed to fill out for the reading tutor I planned on hiring. Her name was Jackie Stanton and I found her online. She had over 20 years of experience in teaching and tutoring kids, teens and adults and we met the day before.

Then it hit me like a slap in the face. I broke out in a cold sweat and my stomach turned, making me feel nauseous. I shut my eyes, but that only brought on the images. Mrs. Taylor. Unbuttoning my shirt after she told me to sit in her desk chair. Unzipping my jeans and tugging them down with my briefs around my ankles. Mrs. Taylor, my English teacher climbing on me, stroking my dick to make it hard. Mrs. Taylor fucking me in that desk chair, moaning and telling me she would give me passing grades if I gave her what she wanted. I was only fifteen.

I shoved away from the kitchen table, knocking my chair over. I fisted both hands into my temples, trying to get the images of Mrs. Taylor out of my fucking head. My phone vibrated on the table, Becky's name lit up on the screen.

"Where the fuk u been? Its fri night. Lets do something!"

The phone lit up again, this time with Brandy texting me pretty much the exact same.

I needed to get shit faced to get those fucking images out of my head. I texted them back to meet me at the Crow Bar. I didn't want to be around my club, or Kat. All I needed were my girls.

* * *

Becky and Brandy were already there as I rolled in on the bike. They were both sitting at the bar, looking down at their phones, their thumbs texting at warp speed. I made my way in between them.

"How's my girls tonight?" Neither one of them looked up from their phones as Grease slid a frosty mug of beer my way.

I gulped half of it down, wiping froth off my lip. Brandy was the first to look up, pouting, "Where have you been, Magnet?"

I pulled her to me, "Sorry babe. Just had a busy couple of weeks. But I'm here now. So, let's get busy catching up, and getting fucked up!"

Brandy giggled. It was high pitched, so different from Kat's.

An hour later the girls had filled me in on their past two weeks as I downed a shot of vodka, trying to look interested in their lives. They worked at some high-dollar designer clothing store that - for the life of me - I could not remember the name of.

My phone sat on the bar and it lit up with Kat's name as it vibrated. I didn't answer. A few seconds later, it lit up again that she'd left me a voice mail.

Becky leaned in, brushing her tit on my forearm, "Are you fucking her, Magnet?"

"No, I'm not fucking her Becky. Cool your jets."

"What does she got that me and Brandy can't give you?"

"She's just a friend for fuck sake!"

"That girl is not into someone like you, Magnet."

"Someone like me, huh? What the fuck is that supposed to mean, Becky?"

"Oh, you know, she likes those intellectual-types. The guys that like to read and do techy geeky shit. You may be fucking her now, but she'll get bored with you after a few months."

"Just like I'm bored with you right about now?"

Becky's brows shot up as I guzzled the last of my beer, and threw a wad of cash on the bar, "See ya, Grease!" I was off my barstool and headed out leaving the B girls sitting there without my dick in their hands. I climbed back on my bike and opened the throttle, and headed to the clubhouse, where I always went. To be with my Chaos brothers.

CHAPTER ELEVEN

KAT

I struggled all day to hold back tears at work as I stood at the front counter, sorting through used books that were brought in by customers over the past week. Noah didn't answer my call the night before, not even a text message. It was my fault. I knew I was smothering him, but I needed to hear his voice every day. When he didn't return my call, it felt like a stab in the heart. Maybe saying those three words to him was too much for him to handle.

I kept looking at my phone, hoping Noah would call me. But by mid-afternoon, there was still no call or text. The jingle of the little bells on the door steered my eyes away from my phone. It was

Becky and Brandy, walking in holding designer store bags.

"Oh, hi Kat!" Brandy smiled, but her eyes didn't.

"Hi Brandy, hi Becky." My voice not as cheery as it usually was when customers walked in.

"So, this is where you work! Me and Becky were out shopping today and wanted to stop by." Both B's appraised the black summer dress I wore. "That's a cute dress! Where did you buy it?"

I gave her similar answer I gave Lillian at Easter, "Oh I bought this at the local Goodwill."

"Well I hope you washed it first before wearing it." Same answer as Lillian too.

I fumbled with the paperback books, trying to focus, as they moved toward me. "Are you looking for a good summer read?"

Becky leaned up against the counter, placing her designer bags on it. "Hmm... Not really."

My phone lit up with Noah's name. It was a text message. They both started to giggle.

Heat crept up my neck to my ears, "What's so funny?"

Becky batted fake lashes, "Magnet was busy with us last night. That's why he never called you back."

"Oh really? And what did the three of you do?"

"We both fucked him!" Her eyes turned into an angry glare, "That's what we did! So back off, Kat.

He's totally NOT into you! Both me and Brandy give him what he needs. He's not very bright."

Brandy snorted, "He's pretty dumb actually."

Becky continued, "He's like a lost puppy dog and that's why he needs us! He'll get bored with you quick. You don't have what it takes to keep a man like him happy."

Just like Lillian, they were jealous! Of me! "You know it's really sad that you fake bitches think you can keep a good man like Noah down. Use him, degrade him, treat him like shit! And I'm amused at the fact that you both feel threatened by me! You both know, in your gut, that Noah is a much better person than the two of you combined!"

Both B's didn't expect Kat's claws to come out as their perfectly tweezed eyebrows shot up.

"Now if you're not here to shop for a book, then get the fuck out of the store."

They huffed, grabbing their designer bags off the counter, and stormed out of the store, the bells jingling loudly.

The moment they disappeared around the corner, I bolted down the romance isle to the back office, slamming the door shut. I pulled my glasses off and broke down crying. The floodgates were opened and all the hurt I tried to swallow down that day suddenly came pouring out. I couldn't hold it back anymore. Then I remembered that Noah had sent me a text before I ran the B's out of the store and I returned to the counter to fetch my phone.

"Coming by to talk." Was all he texted.

It was five pm and I went to the door to turn the store sign over to CLOSED. I wiped tears that streaked down my cheeks with the back of my hand, and sniffled when I heard the pipes on Noah's chopper. He pulled into the parking lot and climbed off the bike, hanging his helmet on the handlebar.

He walked in, and I locked the door. "Hey Kat. Sorry I didn't call you back – "

I didn't even look at him and stomped away, heading back to the office, "I guess you were just too busy fucking Becky and Brandy last night!"

I didn't get too far down the aisle before Noah was on me. He seized my arm, and I spun around to face him, "Where did that come from? I didn't fuck them last night!"

I shrugged him off and headed to the office. He was close behind. I crossed my arms over my chest, "Don't lie to me Noah! Becky and Brandy were just here! They told me you didn't want to answer my call because you were too busy fucking them!"

He looked up at the ceiling, fisting his hands through his hair, "God Damnit! I didn't fuck them, Kat!"

"Then why didn't you call me?"

Noah stepped up to me, clutching my arms as I kept them folded in front of me, trying to shield myself from the pain when he admitted it, "I'm done with them Kat. Both of them. I care about you. I've never felt like I could be myself around anyone until I met you. There were some things I'd done a long time ago. Things I've never told anyone about. Those bad memories all came flooding back to me yesterday when I was trying to fill out the paperwork for the tutor I hired!" His brows knitted together, and I saw the pain in his eyes.

I dropped my arms, "Noah. Did you hurt someone?"

"No. Nothing like that. I'm good now. I did go see Becky and Brandy last night at the Crow Bar. But left them there. I rode over to the clubhouse and pounded a few beers with some of my brothers. I realized that this thing I had with the girls was just that. A thing. I don't feel anything for them. I guess I never really did. I didn't want anything more than fucking because I felt that's all I was good for. You don't make me feel like I'm just a chick magnet. You make me feel like there's more to me. You see that. You see me - Noah."

And at that moment, I claimed Noah as mine. I pushed him with both hands, shoving his back against the wall. I jumped, grabbing the front of his tank and smashed my mouth over his. We both groaned as he seized my thighs, picking me up so they wrapped around his waist, and he carried me to the desk. When my ass landed on the desk, he stepped back and unzipped his jeans. I gathered my long dress, dragging it up slowly. His eyes roamed down to my bare calves and thighs as he fumbled with his jeans and boxers, yanking them down. His immense cock sprung free, bouncing against his muscled stomach. The V-shape of his hips was a beautiful sight. He was like the Greek Myth, Adonis in human form.

I spread my thighs for him. His hand wrenched my panties aside and his rock-hard manhood penetrated my eager wetness. My head fell back, and I cried out, gripping his broad shoulders, as he thrusted into me over and over again, his hips bucking roughly, slapping against me.

Noah growled and nibbled my earlobe, relentless as he drove his bold fullness inside me, "I've wanted to sink my cock deep inside you the moment I caught you in my arms Katrina."

Exhilarating waves of pleasure rushed through my body as I clamped my teeth down onto his shoulder. My scream was muffled as I exploded with a lightening hot orgasm. "That's it, come on my cock!"

My whole body spasmed as Noah continued to fuck me hard on that desk. I shoved him back, his cock glistening wet. I fell to my knees, and gripped his slick shaft, enclosing my lips around it.

He hissed, his hand seized the back of my head. I looked up at him, wearing my glasses. His head fell back, "Fuck!" he yelled.

I tasted my own femininity as I sucked as much of his cock into my mouth, stroking him at the same time. I felt his flesh harden even more and knew he was close to coming, but I kept tormenting him with my lips and tongue.

He fisted my hair, as my head bobbed, "I'm going to explode in that sweet mouth of your Kitten! Are you ready for it?"

"Mm Hmm" I hummed as I took most of him down my throat. My nails dug into his firm ass cheek as he clenched it. He growled and exploded in my mouth, squirting hot semen down my throat.

Noah leaned over me then, bracing his muscular arms on the desk. I rose and sat back on the edge of it. I pulled him down to lay on top of me. "You belong with me Noah."

CHAPTER TWELVE

MAGNET

Fucking Kat on that desk was the sexiest damn thing I'd ever done with a woman. And she wasn't fucking the Chick Magnet, she was fucking *me*. Noah. I saw another side of Kat, the wild and wanton woman, as she looked up at me wearing those glasses, sucking my raging hard dick!

She called her mom letting her know she would be staying with me that night. She followed me back to my house and the moment we stepped inside, our hands and mouths were all over each other, stripping our clothes right in front of the door. I picked Kat up and she wrapped her soft thighs around my waist.

She impaled her tight wet pussy on my hard cock until my balls smacked up against her ass. She clung to me, whimpering next to my ear.

"I'm gonna wreck that pretty little pussy of yours Kitten." I carried her to my couch, laying her down. She spread her thighs for me as I made my way down her luscious squirming body to her pussy, "Now it's my turn…"

She sucked in a breath when I blew over her swollen clit. I ran my firm tongue right up her soft wet heat and watched as she cried out, arching her back, her hard nipples begging for my attention.

She dug her fingers into my hair as she moaned, her hips gyrating in rhythm to my tongue tasting her sweetness. I started to tease her, planting little kisses up and down her pink pussy.

"Please Noah! Fuck me!"

That was all I needed to hear. I positioned myself over her, gripping the back of the couch. I sank into her, filling her up completely. Kat's nails dug into my back, leaving scratch marks as I pumped into her, making her cry out as I thrusted deep and fast.

Moments later, Kat shoved me, and I landed on my back on the hard wood floor. She climbed on top and rode my cock. Our joining was rough and primal, like we were making up for lost time, our grunts and moans echoing though out my house.

We both collapsed on that floor, exhausted, my dick drained. I couldn't remember the last time I felt so sedated. Endorphins spread through our bodies. We steadied our heavy breathing, our bodies covered in sweat. Kat fell asleep, her flushed rosy cheek rested on my chest. I couldn't help but chuckle when I heard her soft little snores.

I grabbed a blanket off the couch and wrapped Kat in it and carried her to my bedroom so she could sleep on something softer than a wood floor. I dozed off too, keeping her soft little body close to me.

We both slept through the night. I quietly climbed out of bed before sunrise to get a shower in before I woke Kat up. But the moment I stood under the shower, she was there with me.

She grabbed the soap, "Let me wash you," and began to lather my chest, my thighs and my cock and balls until I was standing to attention again.

I spun her around. She braced herself, planting her hands against the tiled wall. I seized her hips, nudging the head of my cock right against her wet pussy and nipped at her neck, "You want more huh?"

"Yes!"

I slammed into her warm softness and fucked her hard once again, as the steam from the shower clouded up the bathroom mirror.

* * *

I parked my truck at the job site a bit late, taking my sweet time with Kat in the shower.

"Did you hit the snooze button too many

times? Or did your girlfriends make you late?" Ted, my dad, leaned against the bed of his truck, a large cup of coffee in hand, shaking his head.

I grabbed the hard hat and climbed out of my truck. I still needed to lace up my work boots, "Sorry Pops."

"Aren't those girlfriends a bit too high maintenance son? Why don't you find yourself a nice girl to date? Someone you can bring over to the house for your mom and me to meet?"

I knelt down, lacing up my boots, "Yeah. Well I'm not seeing Brandy and Becky anymore."

"Glad to hear it son. They seemed nice, but you should think about settling down with one woman."

"That's what I need to talk to you about Pops. I met this girl. She's a good friend of the club. She's part of it, actually. She's different than most girls I've banged - I mean dated. I have this connection with her. And to be honest, it scares me a bit."

"You love this girl?"

I looked away from him. "Not sure. It probably won't last anyway. Maybe a few more months. Once she finds out how much of an illiterate man-whore that I am- "

Dad stepped toward me, slapping a hand on my shoulder, "Son, you're a good man. You could be a world class genius like Albert Einstein. But all the smarts in the world won't give you happiness. Sounds like this girl is someone special to you."

I looked down, "Yeah. She's special."

Dad thumped the top of my hard hat "Well, what's her name?"

"Katrina. Kat."

"Then bring Kat over sometime. I'm sure me and your mom would like her."

* * *

"Fuck!" Brandy's car was parked out front of my townhouse when I pulled up in the driveway, and I knew full well they were inside. I'd made the stupid mistake months ago of giving them a key. I walked in the front door to see both of them on my couch, legs crossed, arms crossed. This wasn't going to be good, but I knew it had to be done. End this thing, whatever the fuck this thing was.

"Not doing this anymore. It's over. You have five minutes to get your stuff and leave. I'm replacing the locks so that key won't do you any good after today."

Becky was off the couch. I was quicker, grabbing her arm as she swung back to slap me right across the face. Her eyes bore into mine. I shook my head slowly, "Not gonna happen sweetheart. Now get your shit and get the fuck out of my house."

She yanked out of my grasp and rushed past me and out the door. Brandy was close behind and spit, right in my face. I slammed the door behind her so hard something cracked.

CHAPTER THIRTEEN

KAT

I was prepared for my mother's inquisition as I pulled up in front of my house the morning after I was with Noah. She was sitting on the couch, in her pink bath robe, fidgeting, her knee bobbing over her other leg.

"I'm fine, mom."

She looked down at my dress, "Well I hope so, because the way you're wearing that dress tells me something different!"

I looked down. My dress was inside out and on backwards, the tag staring back up at me. Warmth spread up my neck to my cheeks, to a full-on blush.

I didn't know what to say. I was speechless and

embarrassed in front of my own mother. I jumped when she slapped her thigh and laughed, "Oh Katrina. The look on your face! Priceless!"

My blush suddenly disappeared, and I held my stomach as I laughed along with her. She didn't rake me over the coals about staying the night with Noah. I was a grown woman, and she liked him. He was the first person she called the day that Stuart attacked me. And she knew I was safe with him.

I collapsed onto the couch next to her and let out a deep sigh, my body feeling like I had worked out at the gym for two hours. "I'm in love with Noah, mom."

"I know, sweetie. I could see it when you kept batting your eyes at him at the cookout."

"It scares me sometimes because I told him that I loved him. I didn't expect him to say it back but when he didn't, it hurt."

Mom pulled me close to her and cuddled me, "I'm sure he does love you, Kat. Give him time. It takes men a bit longer than us women to realize it. I see how he looks at you, and how he held you right here on this couch. And I loved watching him knock Stuart's lights out after what he'd done to you -"

A knock came at the door. Mom went to the front window and pulled the curtain back to see who it was. "It's Brett and Sean... A moving truck just pulled up in front of their house. I'll tell them to go away if you want me to hon."

"No. It's ok." I came to stand behind her as she

opened the door. Sean and Brett smiled, their hands shoved in their khaki shorts.

Sean was the first to say something, "Hi Mrs. Stevenson, Kat... We just wanted to apologize for what Stuart had done to you... Me and Brett got him taken off the lease and kicked his ass out of the house." He nodded toward the moving truck. "He's gone, and that truck is hauling his crap out of the house. You won't ever see him in this neighborhood again."

My throat tightened as I choked back tears. "Thank you, Sean. Brett."

"If you want to press charges on him for assault, or if there is anything you need us to do, just ask."

I shook my head. "Thanks. I'm ok."

Brett was the quiet one, but he spoke up then, "Have a good day, Kat, Mrs. Stevenson." They turned and walked back across the street while two men carried a couch up the ramp onto the moving truck.

* * *

I walked on clouds the next few weeks, spending my evenings with Noah at his place, and taking on more responsibility at the bookstore now that Will wanted me to manage it mostly by myself. He knew he could count on me, plus Sam was such a great help, taking on more responsibility as well. I even put a 'Help

Wanted' ad online and posted a sign in front of the store.

Noah met with his tutor, Jackie, a few times during the week. She was patient and understanding, and I was so happy for him. The only people who knew about his tutor were me and his parents. He still felt too embarrassed to tell any of his club brothers, not that they would tease or be cruel to him. It was his pride, and I could understand that. We kept this little secret to ourselves, which made our bond even stronger.

I spent my evenings with Noah, either at his house or he would come over and take me and Mom out for a bite to eat. We'd watch a movie together and my love for Noah grew stronger when he included Mom in on our activities. When I spent nights at Noah's, all we did was have lots of sex like two horny teenagers! I teased him one night playing hard to get, so he'd chase me around his house. He was bigger and faster than me, I'd fake being disappointed when he caught me. He threw me over his shoulder, spanked my ass, and carried me to his bed to ravish me. Sometimes we didn't even make it to his bed, doing it on the stairs, in the kitchen, even in his laundry room!

* * *

It was Saturday night, and Sam worked with me until close. James and Noah were riding their bikes over to pick us up on their way to the clubhouse. I leaned my hip against the front counter and stared off into space, remembering nearly a year ago how I met Sam, here in the store when she came in to apply for the job.

"You look so happy Kat! You're even glowing!" Sam woke me back to the present.

I smiled "Yeah, I'm happy. I was thinking about that day you came in here to apply for the job. And how scary James seemed to me the first time I met him." I laughed, "that big, burly caveman biker with tattoos and a beard treating you like you were the most precious being that ever walked on this planet... And you told me there were bad bikers and good bikers... Do you remember, Sam?"

She smiled "Yes I do. And how you called James when Sid took me. You helped save my life, Kat." She wrapped her arms around me and squeezed tightly as we both started to cry.

"I was so afraid for you, Sam. I don't know what I would have done if something happened to you.... And what it would have done to James. And the whole club."

Sam wiped away tears and laughed, "And I remember the look on your face the very first time you saw Noah, the Chick Magnet. I thought I was going to have to pick your jaw up off the ground for sure!"

Just then we heard the loud rumble of pipes and turned to the store front window as James and

Noah pulled in on their bikes. I had to squeeze my thighs together (like I had done many times before) at the sight of him on his yellow chopper, next to James on his black Harley. They both wore their club vests, displaying their center patch: a grinning skull wearing a Viking helmet above two crossed battle axes. Anyone else would have seen them as intimidating, unapproachable, menacing even. But to me and Sam, they looked hot as hell!

We both squealed like teenagers, locked up the store and hurried out. They both revved their throttles a few times, making all kinds of loud racket in the quiet parking lot.

Noah patted the back-fender pad, "Hop on, Kitten. You're gonna get rode hard and put away wet tonight!"

I grabbed the helmet off the backrest, strapping it on, "Not if I ride you first!" I started to *sound* like a biker chick!

James led, and Noah rode staggered close behind. I clung to him tightly, squeezing his hips with my thighs. His hand came around, grasping my thigh and squeezed back. I was looking forward to hanging with his club and all my girls in the Chaos Coven that night, but I also couldn't wait to be alone with Noah so we could fuck each other's brains out!

Most of the club had just arrived when we pulled into the lot. Everyone was there, Gunner and Fiona, Skully and Tanya, the President, Rocky, with his wife Madge, the matriarch of the Chaos Coven.

Spider was there too, and he pulled me in for a friendly hug, then with a handsome grin he whispered, "Remember, you ever want to make Magnet jealous again, just let me know babe."

I snickered, winking at him, "I'll hold you to that, Spider".

Later that night, the Coven did a round of shots at the bar, all of us girls were getting a bit tipsy. Fiona wobbled a bit to the jukebox, picking out some sexy rock songs that we could all dance to. Sam told me that Fiona taught her some erotic dance moves so she could surprise James and boy, did she! Apparently, James made her walk funny for a week!

Wez showed up later in the night, goading Spider into playing a few games of pool. Magnet and Skully both chuckled, telling me that Wez is terrible at playing pool and would get his ass handed to him, since Spider was one of the best players in the club, including Gunner.

As we all stood around at the bar, Noah caged me in between his muscular arms. Every once in a while, he would rub himself up against my rear, and I would wiggle back, which just got me all excited and wet. And my heart felt like it had wings as he'd bend down and nuzzle my neck, showing me affection in front of his club.

The night would have been perfect if it hadn't been for what happened next. Because that's when Becky and Brandy stormed into the clubhouse.

Madge moved to stand in front of me and

Noah, "Oh, hell no! Get your nasty fake asses out of this clubhouse!"

Becky was brave enough to wave her hand in front of Madge.

But then Noah was there and towered over her, "No Becky. You disrespect me? My club? My tribe? Get the fuck out – the both of you!"

Becky stared daggers pointing at me, "He'll get bored with you quick slut!"

"Hey!" she gasped as Noah gripped her arm. "Don't ever disrespect Kat again. Kat has more heart, brains and beauty than the both of you put together. Now get the fuck out!" Noah growled, an inch from her face, his other hand fisted at his side.

A slow clap erupted from everyone, then high pitched whistles, and hooting and hollering as the two B's turned and stormed out of the clubhouse.

Wez walked up and slapped Noah's shoulder, grasping it, and chuckled. "Well done, brother. About time you kicked those fake ass bitches to the fucking curbside!"

* * *

I met Noah's parents for the first time a week later. He told me so many good things about them and I wanted to dress to impress. I asked him if we could take his truck to his parents' house so that I could wear a nice summer dress.

Noah's eyes roamed down my body as I

climbed into his truck in front of my house, "My parents will love you no matter what you wear, Kat." He leaned over and kissed me. The kiss started out sweet, then suddenly began to get heated, our tongues tasting each other.

He pulled away first, "Don't want to show up with a raging hard on in front of my parents Kitten." His voice low, and strained.

I couldn't help but giggle "OK. I'll give you more of that later." I batted my eyes at him, looking innocent, but he knew what a wildcat I could be when we were alone.

His father, Ted, and his mother, Penny, greeted us at their door with warm hugs and smiles. And I could see that Noah got his ruggedly handsome good looks from his father. I pictured his mother, Penny, starry-eyed and tongue tied around Ted when they were young teenagers in love.

They showed me some of their family photos and one of Noah when he was a teenager in high school that hung on their wall. He was so handsome even as a teenager dressed in his football shoulder pads, wearing his uniform and holding a helmet. "I was good at tackling…" Noah said low, winking.

We sat at their dinner table and chatted. I felt as comfortable as I could be around his parents. They were so kind and had a great sense of humor just like Noah. Both Ted and Penny were close to my mother's age and I had a good feeling they would get along well.

I helped Penny clean up after dinner like I always did with my mom at home, leaving Noah and his Dad at the table, drinking beers and chatting like fathers and sons did.

Penny was a brunette beauty, her hair color just a shade lighter than my own. Noah had her gorgeous blue eyes.

It was getting late, as Noah's parents gave me warm hugs. "You should bring your mother along next time for dinner, Kat. Ted and I would love to meet her." Penny said, making my heart feel like it had wings and wanted to fly. I hugged her back, "Thank you so much Mrs. Davenport -."

"Please, just call me Penny. No need for formal stuff around us, Kat."

"Ok Penny. I'll bring my mother, Jean over for dinner soon."

Then Ted gave me a hug, his height matching that of Noah's and I felt like a dwarf, "Now you keep tabs on Noah. We want him over more often. And now he's got you to keep him on the straight and narrow, Kat."

Noah took my hand as we walked to his truck, "Hey, let's go take a walk. I'll show you around my neighborhood"

He pointed to the house across the street, "That's where Tanya lived and grew up with her parents. And there, in her front yard, is where she kneed me in the balls."

I stopped walking and doubled over laughing.

He tilted his head, "I love your laugh Kat. It's genuine." He wrapped me in his arms and leaned in to kiss me.

We walked to a playground two blocks away from his parents' house. I walked up to the swing set. It was built a long time ago, with old rusty metal poles and black rubber seats that hung from metal chains. "I haven't swung since I was a kid! Will you push me?"

"Sure Kitten."

It was getting dark out and lightening bugs appeared around us, flying lazily, their little bodies glowing yellow, as Noah pushed me on the swing. As Noah pushed me, I leaned back, lifting my legs straight out, then leaned forward, bending my knees when I swung back to him.

"So how are things going with Jackie, your tutor?"

Noah pushed me again, "All right, I guess. She let me choose between a few books to read, so I picked one. She'll come by the house for about an hour once a week."

"Which book did you choose?" I felt I was prying because he seemed like he didn't want to talk about it.

"I chose 'The Chronicles of Narnia." He pushed me again and I swung even higher, the lightening bugs blinking around me.

"Oh, that will be a fun book to read!"

I swung back, but this time Noah grabbed the

chains on the swing, covering my hands with his, and stopped my momentum. "I don't know Kat. This tutoring thing. Not sure it's for me. You can't teach an old dog new tricks. And I'm old when it comes to trying to teach me how to fuckin read!" His voice was low and strained.

I leaned my head back and looked up at him. "Noah, I'm here to for you. Your parents know about your tutoring too and I think it's a very brave thing to do. To learn and grow and get your GED. And I understand when it gets frustrating, but just remember why you are doing this. You want to help your dad and his business. They are proud of you. I'm proud of you."

It wasn't quite dark yet, and as my head leaned back, I could see his handsome smile before he leaned down and planted a kiss on my lips.

CHAPTER FOURTEEN

KAT

The following weekend was girl's night out with the Chaos Coven. It wasn't my first time joining the Coven for some fun but since me and Noah were together, it made it even more special. I felt even closer to Tanya ever since Noah told me stories about them growing up together and how loved each other like brother and sister. I also remember the first time I saw Noah at the clubhouse and how she had warned me to just admire him from a distance because he was a player, the Chick Magnet.

Fiona's brother, Seth, was now prospecting for the club and Tanya's man, Skully was his sponsor. Seth wouldn't get his club name until he was fully patched in, but everyone started calling him Scrapper. From what I was told, Seth and Fiona had a rough upbringing at home with their parents. And Seth ran away but came into town to find his sister again. All anyone knew was that he had lived alone, homeless, on the streets, fighting to survive. Skully also had a tough upbringing as an orphan, going from one foster home to the next. It was only natural to see Skully and Seth quickly form a bond.

Seth even took a motorcycle riding course and got his M-class license. He was still a beginner rider, but he seemed to catch on and fit in well with the Chaos Kings. He bought a used bike from the owner of the motorcycle shop that Skully worked as a mechanic. He rode it that night to follow us as a chaperone, as we all climbed into an Uber van - me, Sam, Madge, Tanya, and Fiona.

We always seemed to find a reason to celebrate and this time it was for my promotion to manager at the bookstore. We stopped in at a nightclub near DC, and grabbed a table, ordering a few rounds of fruity shooters. Sam seemed quiet and she got a bit nauseous sitting in the back of the van, so she wasn't really up to drinking. Fiona's friend, Destiny showed up a bit later, pulling her out on the dance floor. It was the first time I met Destiny, a gorgeous dancer friend of Fiona's, with her exotic features and long black hair. Seth was one step behind, of course, watching over them both, his arms folded and looking so intimidating. He held his stance wide near the dance floor, to make sure no men would try and make a pass or even dance with them.

James kept blowing up Sam's phone with text messages. He was not the insecure jealous type, who tried to keep tabs on her, but he was the protective type, so I found it odd that he would bother her with texts when she was with the Coven. The techno music was loud and thumped through the speakers in the dimly lit club. Strobe lights and disco balls made me a bit dizzy after a few beers and shooters.

Sam touched my elbow leaning over, "James wants us all back at the clubhouse!"

"Is everything ok?"

Sam smiled, "Yeah, everything is ok. James has just been a bit edgy today that's all."

My phone lit up just then with a text from Lillian:

"Jean said you were out tonight. Can I meet you? I need to talk"

I groaned, not wanting to respond, but Lillian had never sent me a text before, so I thought whatever it was might be important.

"Sure. Meet me at the Chaos Kings Clubhouse. I'll be there within the hour"

Madge gathered the Coven, Seth interrupted Fiona and Destiny on the dance floor, and we took an Uber back to the clubhouse within the hour. The Chaos Kings' bikes were on kickstands in the lot as we pulled in, along with James' truck, and I was wondering why he didn't ride his bike.

Sam saw her first as we entered the clubhouse, "Is that your step-sister? Lillian?"

Lillian stood by the bar, her arms folded in front of her, smoking a cigarette. Noah stood next to her, his elbow leaning on the bar. "Yes. She texted me at the nightclub. I didn't know she smoked…"

Wez marched toward me and Sam, his brows knitted. "Your sister just walked in here all by her fuckin self! Don't know if she's naive, brave, or just stupid! She's lucky Magnet and Ratchet knew who she was." I couldn't tell who looked tenser, Lillian or Wez?

I placed my hand on Wez's burly chest, "It's ok, Wez. I told her to meet me here. I knew she would be safe."

As I approached her, she fidgeted with the cigarette between her fingers, flicking ashes in a huge glass ashtray on the bar. Noah greeted me with a huge grin. He picked me up and thrusted his tongue into my mouth, making me tingle between my legs.

"Hey kitten. You taste good and fruity…" He grumbled into my ear. I giggled as he put me down and I turned to Lillian.

She just seemed so nervous, "Hi Kat. I didn't want to just sit in the car out there in the dark. But I don't think your biker friend likes me very much."

"It's ok. That's Wez. He doesn't like a lot of people. So, what do you want to talk about? Is everything ok?"

Her eyes began to well up with tears. Another

surprise coming from her, "I wanted to say I'm sorry. Sorry for being such a bitch and saying those things to you at the cookout a few weeks ago. What I said about your boyfriend, Noah."

"Everything I said was just wrong and hurtful. And other things I've said to you in the past. I know there's no excuse for the way I've acted sometimes. You were right. I have always been a bit jealous of you. "

"Of me?"

"Yes. You're gorgeous and have a warm personality. I felt I had to compete with you when my Dad married your mom. I'm owning up to it now. I hope you can forgive me."

She broke down then and I pulled her to me, giving her a hug. "I accept your apology, Lillian."

She sobbed more, "Thank you Kat. Your mother told me that your neighbor, Stuart, tried to attack you!" She leaned away, looking at Noah, "And how Noah punched his lights out!"

"I would've done a lot worse, but I'd be locked up now, too if I did." Noah's voice tensed, remembering that day.

"I'm ok Lillian. I kneed him in the balls. And Sean and Brett kicked him out of their house."

Lillian rubbed her tears from her cheeks with the back of her hand and smiled "I hope I'm as brave as you if I ever need to be someday, Kat."

"I hope you never have to experience something like that Lillian. Ever! Now cheer up.

You know Noah and you've met James and Sam over there. And now you've met Wez too."

"Ok." She looked down at herself, dressed in a tight black pencil skirt, red blouse and pumps, "I don't exactly fit in here."

"The Chaos Kings are not like that, Lillian. You can be who you are here. No one judges you. They are a great group of people. It's tribal."

Everyone's heads turned to a loud piercing whistle. It came from the President, Rocky, "Turn that jukebox off, Gunner!"

Gunner pulled the plug on the jukebox from the wall and Rocky continued, "Our brother, Ratchet, wants to tell us all something."

Everyone went quiet as James stood on one of the pool tables. He towered over Sam, standing beside him, her arms wrapped around his waist. He looked so huge compared to her, with a wide grin on his face "I got my little Rabbit knocked up! And now I'm gonna marry her!"

The Coven screamed in unison as whoops hoots and hollers came from the Chaos Kings. She was crying, with happy tears as James leaned down and smashed his lips against hers. He jumped down from the table, lifting Sam off, placing her feet on the floor.

Noah seized me by the hips, spinning me around to face him, "It's good when a woman makes an honest man out of a Chaos King huh, kitten?"

Tears of happiness began to swell for me as I

looked into Noah's eyes. He never said he loved me, but I could feel it when I looked into his eyes. He dipped down and brushed a soft kiss against my lips. Innocent at first. I moaned, gripping his hard shoulders, my tongue diving between his lips first.

He gave my ass a loud smack "Now go squeal with the Coven and bring Lillian with you."

I took her by the hand, "Come on Lillian, let's go squeeze the knocked-up bride-to-be! I'll introduce you to my Coven." We rushed over to the circle surrounding Sam, full of squeals and tears of joy.

It dawned on me then why Sam wasn't drinking that night and why she complained about being nauseous in the van – she was pregnant! Shots of anything and everything behind the bar, plus cigars were passed around to the club members, as the Coven drank their own share of alcohol to celebrate.

It was way past midnight as some sobered up enough to ride home or staggered into the rooms down the hall. After a few shots of vodka, Lillian started to relax and after introducing her to everyone, she actually began to enjoy herself. She smiled more that night than I had seen her do in years. I noticed Wez watching her every so often, but he still seemed so tense ever since Lillian showed up.

"I'll be ok to drive, Kat." Lillian started to hiccup, rummaging through her designer purse.

"No Lillian. You should get a ride home. James drove his truck. I'm sure he'd take you home."

She pulled out her keys, "I'm good." She

hugged me, "Thanks Kat. I haven't had this much fun since…I can't even remember!" She giggled and hiccupped again.

Lillian leaned away, spun around a little quickly and planted her face right into Wez's chest. "You're not driving, girl." His eyes glared, snatching the keys out of her hand, "I will. Let's go."

Lillian walked beside Wez, wobbling a bit on her high heels, clutching his huge bicep for balance.

Noah chuckled, "Thanks brother."

"Yeah, Yeah. Fuck." Wez grumbled, as he helped my drunk step-sister wobble to her car.

The clubhouse was quiet. It was just me and Noah. Alone. The next second, Noah grinned, knocking beer bottles and ashtrays off the bar with one sweep of his burly arm. All of it crashed onto the floor behind the bar, as he seized me by the hips, and lifted me up on it. The next moment, our mouths crashed into each other. I moaned, my hands gripping into his hair.

He was over me the next instant, grinding his hips right up against my core. He rose up, unzipping his jeans, "I've been hard for you all night Kat. And I'm not waitin' another second. I'm fucking you right here. Right now!"

I gave myself to Noah so easily, wearing one of his favorites dresses that night. His warm hand caressed my thigh and glided up under my dress. His brows shot up, "Naughty little wildcat" he growled, his eyes full of sexual hunger as his thick finger slid so easily inside me. I cried out. I was soaked. "You're not wearing panties."

I was breathless, unable to speak. I gripped Noah's biceps, needing him inside me. Another bottle crashed to the floor and I cried out as Noah sank himself fully, filling me up with his massive hardness. My fast and heavy breathing matched Noah's as my hips rose in rhythm to his trusts.

"I'm gonna explode all up inside you Kitten. Fill your beautiful pussy with my cum." His voice husky and low.

"Yes Noah!" I screamed out as his cock throbbed, pulsating against my walls. I clung to him tight, as he roared, climaxing and exploding inside me.

We both trembled as waves of pleasure rushed through our bodies. I wrapped my arms around him as he covered me his hulk size. We were breathless.

I clung tightly to him, breathing deep, relishing this moment. I felt his warm breath caress my shoulder, "You're the best thing that's ever happened to me Katrina."

CHAPTER FIFTEEN

MAGNET

My hands gripped the rocky ledge, the rest of me dangling. I couldn't see the ground beneath me. It felt just like being in outer space surrounded by blinking stars. I looked up in the darkness and there was Kat. At first, she was smiling and laughing, but the next minute she was sobbing. I let go of the ledge and reached for her. I wanted to tell her that I loved her, but my grip on the edge slipped and I fell. And kept falling. Through darkness.

I woke up in a cold sweat and I opened my eyes to darkness. I was in my bed. Kat was snuggled up next to me, my arm wrapped around her soft little body. She squirmed and sighed. I didn't wake her. A fuckin bad dream, that's all it was. I climbed out of bed quietly, not waking Kat and trudged half asleep into the bathroom. Going to the sink, I splashed some cold water on my face and stared at the Chick Magnet in the mirror looking back at me.

* * *

I pulled up in front of Jackie's house for my weekly tutoring appointment. I was running behind after work and didn't have time to shower first. My t-shirt clung to me, damp from all the sweat on a hot summer day. I rummaged under my hard hat and found the book before climbing out and ringing Jackie's doorbell.

Jackie answered her door, wearing a fuzzy robe, her eyes and nose looked a bit puffy like she'd been crying. She smiled, "Hi Noah. Come on in."

"Are you sure Jackie? If you're not feeling well, we can do this next week – "

Her nose sounded stuffy, but she waved me in, "No, it's just allergies. Come on in. We'll just sit in my dining room instead of the office."

I followed her to the dining room and took a seat at the table. She sat at the head of the table, crossing her legs, revealing her bare calf. Jackie was an attractive woman and I guessed her age in the mid-forties.

She propped her elbows on the table, "Are you ready to start book two of the Chronicles?"

"Yep", I showed her the paperback, "Bought a used copy of 'The Lion, the Witch, and the Wardrobe' at Kat's bookstore." My chest felt light and my dick stirred in my jeans just thinking about Kat, helping me find the book at her store. It made it more special than just buying one online or downloading it onto some tablet. This one had a few creases in the spine and she told me that's why it's special, because someone else had read it before me.

"Ok, good," She left her chair, "Go ahead and start reading the first chapter - out loud. I'm just going to make me some tea."

"'One, Lucy looks into a Wardrobe. Once there were four children whose names were... Peter, Susan, Ed... Mund. And Lucy. This story is about – "

Jackie's arms came over my shoulders, her hands dipping into the front of my sweaty t-shirt, "You are a fine-looking sexy young man, Noah." She whispered against my ear.

Jackie brushed both her hands down across my nipples, snaking down further. I felt her tits pressed up against my back. "Have you ever made love to an older woman before?"

I pulled her hands out of my shirt. She stepped back as I was out of the chair. She was on me, wrapping her arms around my neck and kissing me.

I shut my eyes and froze. I was sitting in Mrs. Taylor's desk chair all over again. My teenage dick hard as she rode me, the chair creaking and rocking...

I twisted away from her mouth. Seizing her arms, I shoved her away "No Jackie."

"You don't need to pay me for my services anymore. I can teach you to read and you can have my body anyway you want it."

"Fuck!"

She jumped. Her brows shot up, and clutching her robe closed she stepped back, "But I thought... All this time, you've been sending me that vibe Noah!"

I turned, snatched my book off the table and left. Before I climbed back in the truck, I slammed my fists into the door panel, scraping up my knuckles. The rear tires on my truck left burnt rubber as I sped out of Jackie's neighborhood.

* * *

I was sitting at some shit hole bar somewhere far from the Crow Bar and even farther from the clubhouse. It's where I ended up after hauling ass away from Jackie.

I failed at reading, I failed at school, I fucked my school teacher Well...she fucked me, I dropped out of school. I was stupid. I was a total failure at everything.

Kat's name lit up my phone and after few mugs of beer and way too many shots of whiskey, I couldn't talk to her and I was too numb to even answer it. It lit up a few more times. Three voice mails. Then a text.

The girl behind the bar was chewing gum and blew a pink bubble, "You want another shot honey?"

I leaned back, feeling a bit dizzy. My knuckles were raw and I was shit-faced. "Sure. Why the fuck not." I slurred.

Someone wrapped my arm around their shoulder, pulling the barstool out, "Come on, Brother. Taking you home."

* * *

The sun coming through the window made my head throb. I opened my eyes to find myself laying on my couch. Kat laid next to me asleep, snoring quietly. I didn't remember anything from the night before. Except speeding away from Jackie's house and planting my ass on a bar stool to drink myself to oblivion.

Kat mewed and opened her eyes. My throat was dry as a desert. "How did you get me home?" was all I could croak out.

"I called Sam and James and asked where you could have gone other than the Crow Bar or the clubhouse. Wez came with me. He paid your tab, then put you in my car. He rode your bike here to your place." She sat up, her eyes full of sadness, "You wouldn't answer my calls or text last night. What happened Noah? Me and Wez saw the dents in the door of your truck... And your knuckles are raw and bleeding."

I pressed my palms into my eye sockets, "Jackie came on to me. Wanted to trade sex for tutoring me. I turned her down and hauled ass out of her neighborhood. Thank the fuck she didn't call the law on me. You never know what a woman like that has running through her mind."

Kat's head titled, smiling down at me "I love you Noah, and I trust you. You didn't have to go and get yourself shit-faced drunk because of it. You could have told me."

"It's not just that. Remember when I told you I'd done things in my past?"

"Yeah?"

"I fucked my English teacher in high school. Well, she fucked me. I was sixteen. And a virgin. There was another teacher too. Mr. Lorenzo. He didn't fuck me, but he sure did try to get down my pants a few times though."

The look of pain and a bit of anger in Kat's eyes at that moment was like a dagger in the chest. "Oh Noah!" She started to sob, clinging to me then.

"Shh. Don't cry Kitten."

"Have you ever told anyone what happened to you?"

"Nah. Not even the guys I hung with in school. You'd think I would have, but I didn't. Just didn't feel like it was something to brag about. So, there you have it. Wez is right. I am a fucking slut."

Kat gripped my shirt, "Damnit no you are not! You are a man with a huge heart! You were taken advantage of at such a young age, and you didn't brag about it to your friends. Do you think I'm a slut because Stuart attacked me?"

I jumped up "Fuck no!"

"Well then, see? Now forget about Jackie. I don't have a college degree, and no teaching credentials, but I'll help you learn to read Noah."

Tears streamed down Kat's cheeks and I wiped them away, stroking her soft skin. "I would like that." I covered her lips with mine, pulling her into me, gripping her gorgeous dark brown hair into my fist.

CHAPTER SIXTEEN

KAT

It was Bike Week and the club rode in a group, for three hours, taking breaks along the way to the coast. Thousands of people rode in for the event, and the bars were packed and all you could see was leather, jeans, and motorcycles. Vendor tents were set up in parking lots, selling t-shirts, bike parts, souvenirs - anything and everything tailored to bikers. There was nothing like the feeling of riding on the back of Noah's chopper and being part of his club for the week-long event.

The club stayed together and booked rooms at an old motel near the boardwalk. Smelling the salty sea air as we all rode down the main coastal highway, with the sound of thundering pipes all day and all night was exhilarating. I was so turned on, clinging to Noah, feeling so proud of being his ole lady at Bike Week.

The first night, we walked on the beach together, just the two of us. The waves crashed, as the wind whipped through our hair. I took my flip-flops off, padding along the wet sand feeling it smashed between my toes as I walked beside Noah. He held my hand, but stopped, pulling me into his big strong arms, "I would love to make out with you right here on this beach, Kitten." He dipped down and kissed me.

We held each other in silence, listening to the wind and the waves crashing on the sand, feeling like we were the only human beings on the planet.

I could see his handsome smile even in the darkness, the full moon the only light illuminating us. "I've held myself back for too long. To the point that I was going over a cliff. But now I don't care if I fall, because I'm falling hard. I love you Kat. You belong with me."

I swallowed back tears of happiness, "I know."

Spending Bike Week together with the Chaos Kings MC was a happy moment for both of us. Nothing or no one could break us apart. At least that's what I thought.

* * *

After the incredible week we had, I was back in the bookstore with Sam. She gave off that motherly glow as she rung up a customer at the front counter of the bookstore. Just when I thought James couldn't appear any larger next to his Rabbit, he was larger than life, with so much love and pride on his face when he was next to her. You could only feel love when seeing them look at each other.

The Chaos Kings MC packed up the following weekend to ride to the annual Bike Week along the ocean coast of eastern Maryland. Since Sam was pregnant, her and James stayed home, and she helped out at the bookstore, training a new high school kid, Kenny, who needed summer work.

"So, tell me all about Bike Week. I need to live vicariously through you for a while Kat." Sam helped me at the counter as Kenny, helped an elderly woman find the Harlequin Romance section in the store.

"Well you know what they say. What happens at Bike Week stays at Bike Week!"

"Oh, come on Kat! I bet you were probably one of the wildest biker chicks there!"

I never saw myself as a biker chick until Sam just said it. I was light on my feet all week, with feelings of giddiness. When Noah told said he loved me was the highlight of the whole weekend. "Well, I did dance on top of one of the bars with Fiona!"

"Hell yeah!"

"Noah and Gunner, well the whole club, kept

their eyes on us, but you could tell how proud they were. All the other bikers were hollering and whooping, at *their* women! Me and Fiona loved it!"

The little bells on the door jingled just then as Noah walked in. He was still wearing his hard hat, "Hi, Sam. "Kat, we need to talk."

"Is everything ok?"

"No. Not really."

He followed me to the back office and shut the door behind him. I jumped as he pulled his hard hat off, slamming it against the wall.

"Noah! What's wrong?"

"Becky came to the job site today. She's pregnant. It's mine."

I felt the blood drain from my face. My knees almost buckled, like a rug being pulled from under my feet. I staggered back, landing on the desk. "Are you sure?"

"No. I'm not, but I'm going to find out."

I was suddenly clinging to him and broke down.

"I'm sorry, Kat. I sure as fuck didn't plan this, you know that. Becky said she loves me. She wants to be together. For the baby."

"Yes. I know. And you are a good man. You need to do what's right."

"You're the best thing that ever happened to me, Kat. But you deserve so much more than what I can give you."

I pulled away, "What?"

"I love you Kat. I will always love you. You're what's pure in my life. What's honest and true. But I have to let you go." My lips trembled as he leaned in and kissed me so gentle, and then turned and left.

"But you belong with me…"

CHAPTER SEVENTEEN

MAGNET

I held Becky the next day, as she cried, telling her that we'd work this out, and that I was there for her. She blamed her emotional outburst on her hormones, and the pregnancy. I should've gone with Becky to her first doctor's appointment, but she only wanted Brandy there and honestly – I didn't really want to go. It didn't take long for Becky to move into my place. Within a week, she had packed her things and moved out of the apartment she shared with Brandy. And she was back in my bed too.

Becky latched on to me all night the first night and I missed Kat so fucking much my chest hurt. I loved her. And I was falling off that cliff.

Brandy would come by, and we all three ended up in bed together, just like old times. It was a struggle to get my dick hard, but I was quick, getting them both off. I crept out of my bed and jacked off in the bathroom. The only images I had as I squeezed my eyes shut were of Kat, the taste of her lips, her soft skin and the feel of her tight wet pussy. I shot my load in the bathroom sink, remembering her crying out my name as she came on my dick or on my tongue as I tortured and caressed every part of her beautiful body.

I crushed Kat that day, leaving her there alone in that office. The same office we fucked in the very first time. I let go of the only woman who knew the real me. But Kat deserved someone who would be able to give her everything she ever wanted. Not someone like me, a total failure, a whore and a half-wit. I did exactly what Ratchet told me NOT to do. But how can anyone blame me. I wanted Kat the moment she fell into my arms that day in the bookstore.

After one week, I thought the pain would get less but it didn't. Not seeing Kat, touching her, hearing her voice was like an open wound that wouldn't heal. I had to go out after work and get to the clubhouse, to be with my club brothers and to get away from Becky and Brandy.

"But I should be with you tonight Magnet!" Brandy was in a rare mood that Friday night. She stood next to my chopper as I climbed on. Her hip jutted out, her arms folded in front of her, glaring and pouting.

I buckled my lid, put on the shades and started it up. The yellow beast roared to life. "Well you're not riding on the bike. You're pregnant for fucks sake Becky!"

I twisted the throttle and high tailed it out of my neighborhood, chomping at the bit for several shots of whatever poison was behind the bar at the clubhouse.

CHAPTER EIGHTEEN

KAT

Noah took a piece of me with him when he left the store that day. Images came flooding back to me: us on the desk, Noah buried deep inside me as I claimed him as mine; the look on his face as he came in my mouth that first time. I fell to the floor and began to cry. Sam watched Magnet hurry out of the store. I saw the look on her face as I dragged myself out of the back office. She was worried. I collapsed into her arms and told her what happened. She agreed to cover my shift so that I could go home.

I rushed home just so I could cry in my

mother's arms. All I wanted to do was sleep in my bed. My mother held me tight and soothed me as I sobbed uncontrollably.

I didn't know it then, but I fell in love with Noah the first time I laid eyes on him. My heart was doomed from that moment on. But how can you deny what your heart wants? Even when you know that your heart will break? I was empty inside. I couldn't eat anything. How could I? Noah had that charismatic aura surrounding him and he made my heart skip a beat every time. I was breathless when I kissed and touched him.

All week long I held onto my phone, hoping and wishing Noah would call or text. He never did.

Lillian took me out for happy hour to a bar just outside of Washington DC, where business, IT, and sales people went after work. We were surrounded by people dressed in suits and pencil skirts. I drank martinis (Lillian's favorite) with her in an attempt to numb myself from the pain.

"Kat, I'm really, really sorry about what happened… I don't even know what to say." I was grateful for Lillian's recent change of heart and was even beginning to like this new and improved version of my stepsister.

"Thanks Lillian."

"Who is this woman anyway? I highly doubt she has any class. At all."

"Her name is Becky. She hates me. I never cared, of course. She staked her claim on Noah way before I came into the picture. I guess she finally won."

"She did not win, Kat!" Lillian's eyes burned with fire, revealing another side of her I'd never seen before. "Noah loves you! This Becky chick thinks she can dig her claws into him by getting pregnant? She knows he's a good man and wouldn't abandon his child so she did the most horrible thing a woman can do to a man: she trapped him!"

I felt like an empty shell, and the only thing inside me was sadness. After a few martinis, those feelings of emptiness turned into anger. "I hope he hurts just as much as I do right now!"

"I think I know a way to make Noah open his eyes and realize that he made the wrong choice."

"How?"

"Make him jealous Kat! That gets them every time."

"I don't know how to play that game."

Lillian smirked and rubbed my arm, "I'll teach you, sis."

* * *

I was dressed in jeans and boots as I waited in front of my house for Wez to pick me up on his bike. I was so nervous because I had only ridden with Noah. I smiled as Wez pulled up on his black Harley and planted his feet down. He twisted the throttle, revving the engine a few times and smirked. "Hop on darlin!"

I strapped on the new helmet I bought a few days ago, plus my shades and climbed on behind him. The pad I sat on was similar to the one on Noah's chopper, but everything else about Wez's motorcycle was different. Wez's bike was painted a flat black with red wheels and high handle bars. "HARDCORE" was painted in gothic letters on both sides of his tank.

I wrapped my arms around his waist, "If I forget to tell you, thank you having me ride along with you Wez!"

He patted my hands that were pressed against his hard stomach, "No problem Kat. It's a brilliant idea. Now let's go make Magnet wake the fuck up!"

After drinking a few martinis with Lillian, we called Sam and told her about our plan. Ratchet had no problem getting Wez on the phone to ask if he was up for it too. As Wez pulled up into the clubhouse lot with me riding on the back, all eyes turned to us. But the only reaction I wanted to see was Noah's.

It had been two weeks since I last saw him. His eyes bore into both me and Wez the moment we pulled in. "I think we got the reaction we were hoping for, darlin'." Wez grumbled to me as he kicked his stand down and I climbed off.

By the time my helmet was off, Noah was there, and he punched Wez right in the mouth. Wez wiped his bloody lip with the back of his tattooed hand and grinned, "I hope that was the best you can do brother, cause that's the last one your throwin'."

"Stop! Noah! I asked Wez if I could ride with him!"

He turned to me his lips flat, his eyes glaring, "Did you fuck him too?"

I shoved him, but he didn't move, "How can you even say that to me!" I spun and marched toward the clubhouse.

He caught me by the arm, spinning me around, "Goddammit Kat!" I was suddenly lifted up off my feet with my stomach landing on his broad shoulder. "We need to talk. Right fucking now!"

I heard clapping and chuckles from Noah's brothers as he carried me to the same room he carried me in before. Placing me back on my feet, he slammed the door and stalked toward me. I couldn't move. He shoved me against the wall. He pinned my arms up above me, slamming his hips into my stomach, "I don't want to EVER see you on another man's bike! Ever!"

I held my chin high, glaring back at him, "Why the fuck not?"

"Because you belong to me!" he smashed his mouth on my lips hard, as his big hand wrapped into my hair, and pulled to drive his tongue into my mouth, devouring me, claiming me.

I couldn't breathe very well, but I my voice was loud and clear, "I do belong to you Noah!"

He stepped back, pulling his shirt over his head.

We both stripped as fast as we could. Noah bent over and grabbed the backs of my thighs. I wrapped them around his waist as he shoved me against the wall again and drove his fully hardened length up inside me. I cried out at the exhilarating feel of his thick hardness filling me up.

He bucked his hips, thrusting inside me over and over again as I dug my fingernails into his back. Our bodies were one as we grunted and moaned. He growled and I felt his hot come shoot against my cervix, "I love you Katrina!"

I was still impaled on Noah when hooked his arms up under my ass and carried me to the bed, and covered me with his sweaty body, his heart pounding hard against my chest. His cock began to harden again, "You mean everything to me Kat. I promise you I'll never let you go, ever again!" I cried out his name as he thrusted hard into me, savoring the moment as we were joined as one again.

CHAPTER NINETEEN

MAGNET

I held Kat's luscious body, glistening with sweat, close to mine as she clung to me in the bed. My dick finally settled down after exploding in her twice already. I was the first to climb out of bed and put on my clothes. Kat pulled the blanket up to cover her gorgeous tits. She sighed. "Where are you going? Let's stay here a few minutes longer, Noah."

I gathered up my shirt and jeans off the floor, pulling them back on. "Gotta go out there and make it right. I need apologize to Wez, Kitten. You don't take a swing at your own brother. I was wrong."

Kat pouted, "Ok. I understand. It was my

fault in the first place. But that was the only way."

I came down to cover her again, "I know Kat. I'm sorry. You opened my eyes. The moment I saw you on the back of Wez's bike, it tore me up inside. Made me angry. And I was only angry at myself. For hurting you the way I did."

She rubbed her soft cheek against my shoulder, "Apology accepted. Now you see that we belong to each other. That's all I wanted. I'm here to support you, and to help you with your baby any way I can. We have Tanya and Skully too. We can learn from them. You see how they make his son Jake so happy."

I rose off her, sitting back, raking a hand through my messy hair, "The baby. It still hits me in the gut. Me? A dad?"

Kat propped herself up on her elbows, the sheet falling down, to display those tits for me again. "You're going to be an amazing father Noah. That charismatic energy you have will also shine through your son or daughter. I really believe that."

"Well there's some things I need to fix around me, before I can make this work for the both of us."

"I know that. And I still want to help you reach those goals we talked about. Do you remember my neighbors Brett and Sean?"

"Yeah? What about them? They haven't bothered you have they?" My blood pressure rose a bit remembering when that douche bag Stuart attacked Kat.

"No, they kicked Stuart out and came over to apologize to both me and Mom for what he'd done. Brett is actually a high school teacher Noah. He told me the invitation is open if you wanted to tutor with him, and he can help you get your GED!"

I kissed her on the nose and climbed back out of bed, "We'll talk about it later. Cover up those nice tits, Kitten," I went to the door and opened it, "Let me go make peace with Wez and I'll take you home."

Wez slammed his knuckles into my shoulder pretty hard, but I owed him that, then we shared a few shots together. "Never seen you that fuckin' pissed! But that was the reaction we were both shooting for."

I slammed my glass on the bar, "Well thanks Wez." I looked over at Skully, "Pour me another shot. I'm taking Kat home and then I'm dealing with Becky."

* * *

I rode Kat back to her house, then headed back to mine. I no longer felt that sharp pain in my chest. Kat was mine and there was no way in hell I would ever let her go again. My mind was clear about what I wanted with Becky, now that I was honest with myself. I didn't love her and I never would. I loved Kat. The best we could all do was take one day at a time, and do the right thing for the baby when it was born.

But the moment I walked into my house, Becky was sitting on the couch, hugging a pillow and crying.

I had become target practice, as she threw the pillow directly at me, "How can you just leave me alone every night to go get shitfaced at the clubhouse!"

I caught the pillow, and dropped it on the floor. "I'm not shitfaced. We need to talk, Becky." I sat down on the couch next to her, "You living here is just not going to work."

Becky's eyes turned from a fiery stare to shock, "What's that supposed to mean?"

"That means that you should move back in with Brandy. I don't love you. I love Kat."

She clutched her stomach, "But what about our baby? I'm not getting an abortion Magnet!"

"I don't want you to. And I will be there for the baby and help you in any way I can. But there is no you and me anymore."

Becky's lower lip began to tremble, "What does Kat have that I don't?"

I pulled her to me. The three of us had some good times, and even though it had been a rough few weeks with her living at my house, it was still the end of us. "It's not that at all. People change Becky. I've changed."

Becky shoved me, leaping off the couch, "Maybe you'll get lucky and I'll have a miscarriage!" she turned, rushing up the stairs.

I groaned. There was nothing I could say to

make it easy for Becky. I could hear her, loudly stomping around my bedroom, and pulling out dresser drawers. A few minutes later she hurried back down the stairs holding a few bags of her clothes and some sandals, "I'll go to the courthouse this week to fill out the paperwork for child support." Then she left, slamming the door so hard, I heard something crack.

CHAPTER TWENTY

KAT

That heavy weight of pain and anger suddenly disappeared the moment we claimed each other again that night in the clubhouse. Magnet rode me home on his bike and called me after he broke it off with Becky. We knew it wouldn't be easy but at least Becky left without hitting him or spitting on him.

Sam laughed, as she sat directly across from me in the back of the bookstore office the next day, "James said I should have seen the look on everyone's face - especially Noah's - when you pulled up sitting on the back of Wez's bike!"

I got the go-ahead from Will to buy a new monitor for the computer in the back office and was tapping away at the keyboard learning a new accounting app. I smiled, remembering Noah as he buried himself inside me on that very desk, not far from where Sam was sitting now. "Yeah, well it sure did get his attention! He even punched Wez right in the mouth!"

Sam's brows shot up, "Really? OMG!"

"He did apologize to Wez though. Everything is good between them. I just didn't realize that sitting on another man's bike can really piss a man off!"

"Especially if that man is a biker, Kat. That's just one of those caveman territorial things that can start fights, and can even start a war between outlaw clubs."

Lillian appeared in the doorway, dressed in her usual style, all business with a hint of sex appeal. "So? Did the plan work? I couldn't get any details out of your biker friend, Wez."

I laughed "Yes it did work! I got Noah's full attention that's for sure! Did you go see Wez before you came here?"

"Yes. I got the address to his tattoo shop and went by there to see what it looked like. I'd never been inside one before. Wez is definitely *not* a people person. The minute I walked into his shop he copped an attitude with me. He's very intimidating - don't you think?"

"Wez is a good guy. It just takes longer for

people to warm up to him." Sam knew him better than we did.

She looked so beautiful being pregnant, and I realized how self-centered I'd been lately, not sharing in her happiness. "So enough about my drama. How are you feeling with your pregnancy Sam?"

She looked down and touched her stomach, "Well I get some nausea in the morning and sometimes I'm running to the bathroom to vomit my breakfast before I get the work. It comes and goes. The doctor checked me out and other than the morning sickness, everything is just...well...perfect!"

I choked back a tear, gazing at Sam's beautiful glow. She has been through so much in her life: abused and treated like property when she was with the Hell Hounds. Then James comes along - her big burly knight on a black shining motorcycle – and saves her life! He has protected and cherished her ever since. James looks even larger, the proud father and husband-to-be!

"Yeah, and he drives me bonkers sometimes! He treats me like I'm his fragile little bunny! He knows I don't break! And I like it when he's a bit on the rough side... If you know what I mean." She winked and Lillian and I both started to laugh.

"Well, I have to get to my next appointment for a house showing. Hopefully I'll get a buyer today!" Lillian blew us both kisses and left. She was a perfectionist when it came to her career as a real estate agent and she was damn good at it, too.

Sam and I closed the store together and I drove to Noah's house that night. He left the door unlocked for me so when I heard the water running, I rushed up his stairs, stripped off my clothes and surprised him in the shower. He was hard for me instantly, as our hands groped and squeezed each other's bodies. Our tongues franticly licked and tasted each other until Noah spun me around. I slapped my hands against the tiled wall and bent over a bit, arching my back so he could position his thick bulging head against my center. He grunted as he entered me with one hard thrust, and I cried out his name.

By the time we both exploded in frenzied orgasms, we were surrounded by a thick fog of steam from the shower and laughed when we looked at our water-soaked pruney fingertips. I sat in his bed, wearing one of his huge t-shirts, and dried off my hair with a towel. Noah walked around in his boxers that hung low, revealing that sexy V-shape of his hips. I had to look away and watch whatever was on the TV as a distraction because I was tempted to yank those boxers down and suck him off!

He was cleaning up after the mess Becky left, putting things back into his dresser drawers. "So, tell me more about this neighbor of yours."

I sat up, "Brett? Yes, he's a high school teacher. He teaches History and U.S. Civics to freshman. He's about your age." I was so hopeful that Noah would be open to at least meeting him.

His back was turned, rummaging through one of the drawers, "And you told him about me? That I can't read worth a shit and that I'm a high school drop-out?"

I climbed off the bed and rushed to wrap my arms around him, laying my cheek against his broad back, "I wish you would stop saying things about yourself like that. You're a very smart man. Do you know why?"

He turned around, his brows furrowed, wrapping his arms around me, "Why is that, Kitten?"

"Because you made the smartest decision by choosing ME instead of Becky, that's why!"

His head fell back and he started to laugh, making me all tingly between my thighs again.

"You got that right! You're all mine. My sexy little wild cat!"

CHAPTER TWENTY-ONE

MAGNET

It was Friday and I was ready for the weekend. My phone lit up with a text as I climbed on the chopper. My dick was semi-hard thinking about getting between Kat's legs later that night. I hoped it was her texting me, but it came from Brandy, "Please meet me at the Crow Bar - Important"

I grumbled, replying back, "on my way"

I pulled into the lot at the Crow Bar and spotted Brandy's parked car instantly. I walked in to see her sitting at the bar alone, smoking a cigarette. I grabbed the stool next to her.

When she turned to look at me, I saw a dark

purple bruise on her left cheek bone. No amount of make-up could cover a shiner like that. "Who's the fuck-sack that hit you?"

I could tell she'd been crying because mascara stained her wet cheeks. She smashed her cigarette out in an ashtray and reached for me. She buried her face into my chest and began to sob.

I wrapped my arms around her, "Shh. It's ok, Brandy. Tell me."

She pulled away and hiccupped, "Thanks for coming, Magnet." She wiped her nose with a bar napkin.

"Sure. You can tell me what's important after you tell me who the fuck hit you!"

She looked directly into my eyes, "Becky is not pregnant."

A cold chill climbed up the back of my neck and I just stared back at her, "Say that again?"

"She's not pregnant. She never was. She lied to you." Brandy cried out, clinging on to me again, "I'm sorry Magnet!"

"That cunt!"

"Is everything ok on that side of the bar Magnet?" Grease was there, sliding me a full mug of beer.

"Yeah. Yeah. She's just having a fucked-up day." I took several gulps.

I turned back to Brandy. "I guess Becky could have pulled it off too. But for how long? If she's this fuckin' crazy to lie about being pregnant, who knows what else she will do."

She wiped her cheeks again with another bar napkin, "She was so jealous of Kat and hates her with a passion! She tried all she could to drive a wedge between you two. And she spotted you at Bike Week a month back."

"You two were there?"

"Yeah. She was angry that you took Kat along instead of us. She got totally shitfaced one night and met some bikers there too…." Becky reached for her pack of cigarettes and lit another one, "These bikers are not like you and the Chaos Kings, Magnet. They're the bad sort. Meth-heads."

I lifted her chin to look at the bruise, "One of those pieces of shit gave you that bruise too, didn't they?"

She titled her head away, taking another drag of her cigarette, "Yeah. One of them did. There are more bruises. You just can't see them."

"God dam piece of shit!" I roared, wanting to slam my fist into something, or someone. I shot out of my bar stool and pulled my phone out to call Wez.

"Yeah." Wez mumbled.

"Becky faked it. She's not pregnant."

"The fuck?"

"Yeah, I'm with Brandy right now. She just told me."

"That cunt!"

"Yeah, that's what I said!"

"Un-fucking-believable!"

"Got a situation too. Some new dirt-bag friends of Becky's beat up Brandy. Wanna help me out and beat on them a bit too? I really need to smash my fists into someone right about now!"

"Sure man. Should I bring the cattle prod?"

"Nah. Just your fists. It'll be fun. Meet me in fifteen at the Crow Bar."

"I'm there, bro."

I went and sat with Brandy and waited for Wez, "Where do these fuckers hang out at?"

She crushed her cigarette out, "At the Steel Cage…"

"That club reeks of the Hell Hounds MC!"

"Yeah, I know." Her eyes were puffy, but at least she stopped crying, "Magnet, will you tell Kat that I'm sorry? About all of this? I'm kicking Becky out of my apartment too. I'll have to figure out the rent situation, but Becky has gone off the rails! And I sure as shit don't want to be around those meth-heads anymore."

"Sure Brandy. And thanks for telling me all this."

* * *

Thirty minutes later, I pulled into the lot of the Steel Cage with Wez. Brandy gave me a pretty good description of these guys - one had long dark hair tied back with an unkept beard. Another one had greasy messy dark hair and a front tooth missing. We kicked our stands down on the bikes, and strolled right into the club. Strobe lights pulsed as we walked through a thick cloud of smoke, from cigarettes and cigars. I measured up the bouncer, who was about the same size as Ratchet. We scanned the small round tables as loud thumping music blared from the speakers.

One of the exotic dancers swung her hips to the beat on the front stage. There was no way I could miss Becky, with her platinum blond hair and her cut-off jean shorts, showing off her ass cheeks. She was next the stage, shoving some bills in the dancer's thong when she turned and spotted us striding right over to her.

The two meth-heads sat at one of the little tables and their heads turned in our direction. We were only a few feet away when they rose from their chairs. I gripped the long haired one by his dingy jean vest and slammed my fist into his nose. I let go as his head flew back and he landed on the table behind him. Beer bottles crashed onto the floor. I heard Becky scream. I caught Wez out the corner of my eye throwing a few hard jabs at the greasy-haired fucker.

The loud music cutoff right then, and the DJ barked into a microphone from behind a booth, "Hey man! Take that shit outside! We hate having to clean up after you fucking assholes!"

Me and Wez didn't need to waste anymore of our energy on them, but it just felt good to bash our knuckles into something that needed hitting. Wez headed for the door, but I wasn't done with Becky.

Not yet.

She stood there frozen, her eyes bulging out of their sockets. I strolled over to her, my face an inch away from hers, "Brandy told me! You were never fucking pregnant! Stay away from me, stay away from Kat and stay the fuck away from my club! I know Brandy got those bruises from these two fuck-wads. If I ever see another bruise like that on Brandy again? I'll bring Ratchet over here next time and he'll be taking some of their body parts with him."

I snorted up some phlegm and spit it in her face, "Cunt!"

Her head flew back and then she screeched at the top of her lungs. I strolled out of there, hopped on my chopper and followed Wez as we burned rubber at full throttle out of the parking lot.

* * *

Wez headed back to his place and I pulled up in front of Kat's house. She saw the look on my face and pulled me to her when she opened the door, "I knew something must have happened."

I held her tight. Her mother stood behind her, looking as worried as Kat. "I need to tell you something. And Jean needs hear this too."

Kat looked up, her eyes watery, "Do we need to sit down for this?"

"No." I lifted her chin and smiled "Becky's not pregnant. She never was."

Her brows lifted, "Oh my god!" She smiled back, "Really?"

"Yes. I just went to see Brandy tonight and she told me. Becky lied about being pregnant. Just so she could fuck up – ", I looked at Jean, "Sorry... Just so she could put herself between us. I brought Wez along and we found Becky. She's hanging out with a couple of meth-heads. I told her to stay away from you, me, and the club."

"That bitch!" Jean barked.

"Well I called her something much worse." I grasped Kat by her arms, "I made sure I wasn't followed back here, but I want you to stay alert where ever you go, Kat. Be aware of your surroundings. Becky knows where you work, and I don't trust her or those meth-heads. You call me immediately if you ever feel weirded out about anything! Understand? I don't care if I'm at a job site, I'll leave in a heartbeat. I don't want anything to happen to you. Or your mother."

"Yes, Noah. I understand."

I pulled both Kat and Jean to me and held them both. Love can also bring on the fear. Because for the first time in my life, I actually was afraid. Afraid of losing the only woman I'd ever loved.

CHAPTER TWENTY-TWO

KAT

I'd always been a pretty rational person and anger is an emotion that can be irrational. But I've never felt so much anger at one person like I did toward Becky. And some of my anger was also directed at Noah sometimes too. Only because I felt I needed to lash out at him for getting himself involved with a woman like that! I also realized that deep down I had been competing with both Becky and Brandy for Noah's attention. But not anymore. I had my insecurities just like everyone else, but I showed Noah my true self. And he fell in love with me, and that made our love for each other real.

Becky tried to destroy us, but we worked together to put it in the past and move on with our lives. I did as Noah told me, to stay aware of my surroundings at the bookstore or anywhere else I went. His brow was furrowed at times, showing his apprehension that Becky would do something crazy and take it out on me. It was a bit unnerving to think Becky would do something irrational, but Noah told me to never under estimate someone else's thinking, especially if they were angry.

Noah was so protective of both me and my mother, which made us feel safe. He, along with Wez, told the club to stay on the look-out if Becky or those two assholes she hung out with came around. A week had past, but the feelings of anxiety were still there, nagging me in the pit of my stomach.

A month had past and the nag in my stomach settled down a bit, as I stayed close to Noah, to my Mom and the women in the Coven. Noah told his parents that Becky was never pregnant, and they were so relieved and delighted that we were back together again. After all we went through in such a short span of a lifetime, our bond became even stronger. We were there for each other, the club, and our families.

* * *

Noah was reluctant to meet with Brett about helping with his tutoring. I understood his hesitation because of all the unpleasant, and traumatic experiences he endured in high school, and his recent encounter with Jackie.   But he was determined to reach for his goals.

We met Brett for dinner and drinks and chatted at a local restaurant with a comfortable atmosphere. And after a few beers, Noah and Brett actually clicked really well! They opened up to each other and began to discuss the   goals Noah wanted to achieve in ramping up his reading skills to get his GED.

Brett was very laid back and easy to talk to, "We'll start off by reading 'Harry Potter and the Philosopher's Stone'. It's one of my favorites about fuckin wizards and magic!"

Noah chuckled, "Sure. Sounds good."

Brett took another gulp from his frosty mug of beer, "Maybe you can help me out with something too."

"Yeah? What's that?"

Brett's eyes moved to Noah's shoulders and biceps, then looked down at himself, patting his gut, "I really need to get back into shape. Do you think you could be my work out partner?"

Noah's eyes immediately lit up and he grinned "Sure man, I'll work out with ya! I'll text you details on the gym I go to and get you a free pass for the month."

"Deal!" Brett reached out his hand and Noah shook it. And a new friendship was made that night.

* * *

One evening, that nag that was one a small pebble became a heavy rock that sunk to the pit of my stomach when I walked into the front door of my house. There, I saw my mom, sitting on the couch, her eyes wide with fear. Two filthy looking men, sat on either side of her.

Becky stood by the couch, holding a revolver. It was pointed it at me. "Come on in Kat! The party is just starting!"

I felt a hot, fiery rage building up inside me, as one of the assholes sitting too close to my mother draped his arm over her shoulder.

"GET YOUR FILTHY FUCKING HANDS OFF MY MOTHER!"

I took a stepped forward, but Becky kept the gun pointed right at me, "I'm the one with the gun bitch. So, I call the shots!" Becky screeched.

The piece of shit with the missing tooth kept his arm wrapped tightly around her, letting out a high-pitched giggle, "These bitches better have some cash hidden around here somewhere!"

Becky turned to him, "We'll get to that soon enough. You can rip this house apart if you want, I don't give a shit!" Her eyes pivoted back to me, "But first, you WILL call Magnet and tell him to get his ass over here!"

Her hand that held the gun began to shake. In that moment, all I wanted to do was drop kick her right between the legs "You tell your scab friend to get away from my mother, and then I'll call him."

"I'm ok Kat. Just call him." My mother, the brave lioness, kept her eyes only on me.

I pulled out my phone pushed Noah's name. He answered in just one ring, "She's there isn't she Kat?"

"Yes. With a gun. Her friends are here too."

"If they hurt you or your mother, they're all dead. Be there in ten."

I hung up. My eyes glared at Becky "He'll be here in ten minutes."

Just then the doorbell chimed. Becky steered the gun to the door. I knew it could only be Brett from across the street, "It's ok. It's just my neighbor." My voice shook, trying to keep Becky calm with that gun.

"Tell him to go away!" Becky barked, hiding the gun behind her.

I moved to the door and opened it. Brett's smiled faded the moment he saw the look on my pale face. He leaned over my shoulder. His brows turned downward, when he saw Becky, and he lowered his voice, "Everything okay Kat?"

"Uh. Yeah. Just a few of Noah's friends. He'll be here in ten minutes." I faked a smile, my throat dry.

"Well. Ok. I'll come back later."

The sinister looking man with the long beard scooted away from my mother. He patted the couch and grinned at me, "Come and sit by me, little pussy cat."

Bile rose up my throat as I walked over and sat next to him. He chuckled, wrapping an arm around me. He smelled of body odor and cigarettes. At least I was wedged in between one of those disgusting assholes and my mother.

I stared at the clock above the TV, watching the long hand move ever so slowly. Becky paced back and forth biting on her long acrylic thumb nail, her eyes darting around the room.

I breathed a sigh of relief, realizing I was holding it as three knocks came at the door, "Becky, It's Magnet. I'm coming in!"

The door knob turned slowly and Noah stepped inside, leaving the door ajar. His hands were raised and he kept his eyes on Becky who now pointed the gun at him. "Just take it easy with that gun, Babe. It's me you want. Just let Kat and Jean leave the house and we'll talk."

Becky's hand shook as she leveled the gun at Noah's chest. Her bottom lip started to tremble, "I was the best god damn woman that ever came into your life! You loved me more than you ever loved Brandy! Then you just threw both of us out of your house for" she looked down at me, "this frumpy bitch!"

Noah took one step toward her, tilting his head slightly, "I'm sorry babe. I'm a Chick Magnet, remember?" His eyes turned soft, taking another step, "You're right. I'll get bored with Kat sooner or later."

Becky lowered the gun a bit and began to sob. Noah was then only inches away from her. He raised her hand to point the gun into the middle of his chest.

"Noah! Please don't!" I cried out.

He kept his eyes on Becky, holding her hand that still kept a shaky grip on the gun. "Do you really want to kill me Becky? After all the good times we've shared? You know we can still be together right?"

Her head dropped. In half a second, Noah snatched the gun out of Becky's loosened grip and shoved her hard against the wall face first. He pinned her there, as Wez and James rushed in through the front door, stampeding toward the two men on the couch and my mother screamed. We both jumped off the couch and out of the way as the Chaos Kings began pounding their fists into them.

Brett must have called the police, because a minute later, came the blaring sounds of sirens. Three police officers came through the door, followed by Brett. Two officers pulled Wez and James off the meth-heads, their faces a bloody mess. Noah left Becky to the third officer, keeping her pinned against the wall, and restraining her wrists in handcuffs as she screamed and sobbed.

My mother sobbed, clinging to me tight as Noah came to wrap his arms around us both, "Are you ok? Did they hurt you?"

"We're ok Noah." I released my mother so she

could stay in his arms. "Hold her." I moved quickly toward the officer who jerked Becky away from the wall. And with all my strength I had, I back handed her hard across the face! She cried out as Wez braced his hands on my shoulders pulling me back to him and chuckling, "Whoa there Kat. We don't want you riding along with her to the pokey now do we?!"

EPILOGUE

KAT

I sat on my couch, changing the channel on the remote to check on the weather forecast that night as my mother paced back and forth in front of the window in the living room. "You look fine Mom. Stop fidgeting or you're going to wear out that carpet."

She stopped and looked down at herself dressed in jeans, a cute sleeveless blouse with pink flowers and brand-new motorcycle riding boots, "Is this appropriate enough? Should I change into something different?"

"Yes, you're dressed appropriate enough, looking like a hot sexy biker mama!"

She giggled "Oh stop Katrina. It's just a ride on a motorcycle with Noah's work friend, Hank. It's not a date."

"Oh yes, it is a date Mom!"

That's when we heard the rumble of pipes outside. She rushed to the front window peering out behind the curtain.

"Don't go out there, Mom! Make them come to the door and greet us. I want to take a look at Hank myself!"

The doorbell rang and I got to the door and opened it before her. Noah leaned against the frame, with a handsome grin on his face. "Hey Kitten." He nodded his head to the older man standing next to him. "This is Hank".

Hank had head full of salt and pepper hair, with a full growth of beard. He nodded, "pleasure to meet you, Kat." His eyes pivoted from mine to my mom, standing right behind me, "You must be Kat's sister?"

She giggled and stepped around me, holding her hand out to the huge burly man. "I'm Kat's mother, Jean."

Hank clasped her little hand in his huge paw-like grip, "Well the pleasure is all mine darlin. I mean Jean."

I smiled up at Noah as Hank and Mom chatted, like two nervous teenagers going out on their first date. Hank was close to my mother's age and was a widower, who worked for Noah's father's business. We thought they would be a good match for a blind date to the county fair that night. Hank also rode a Harley – the kind with all the bells and whistles, with a fairing, hard saddle bags, and even a radio and cd player. It was painted in pearl white, parked next to Noah's chopper.

Noah pulled me into his chest, wrapping his strong arms around me and planted a warm and not so chaste kiss on my lips "You two biker chicks ready to ride the ferris wheel tonight?"

My lips lifted to a devilish grin, looking up into his sea blue eyes, "Ready to be rode hard and put away wet, Chick Magnet!"

THE END

ABOUT THE AUTHOR

Linny grew up in Northern Virginia, right outside Washington DC, self-published her debut novel, "Salvation in Chaos" in January of 2018. Her stories are about scruffy, sexy alpha bikers who belong to a tribe, their club, and the women they fall in love with. They live in a world full of chaos, not unlike reality. But within that chaotic world, they live their lives the best way they can and discover true love.

SOCIAL MEDIA

Facebook page:

https://www.facebook.com/Linnylawlessromance

Chaos Coven Clubhouse:

https://www.facebook.com/groups/1481551685255

429

Website:

https://linnylawless.com

Instagram:

https://www.instagram.com/linnylawless

Goodreads:

https://www.goodreads.com/user/show/73729078-

linny-lawless

BookBub:

https://www.bookbub.com/authors/linny-lawless

Made in the USA
Columbia, SC
18 October 2018